Praise for McMullen Circle

"These deeply literary, heartfelt, and heartbreaking characters call to mind the work of Elizabeth Strout, Gail Godwin, and Richard Russo, but Heather Newton is her own writer. Her characters are shot through with longing and hope, and in this small community we watch as big dreams and big desires are dreamed and felt, run toward and away from. This is the kind of book that readers return to to reemerge themselves in Newton's world, and it's also the kind of book that writers return to to see how she pulled it off."

—Wiley Cash, author of *A Land More Kind Than Home*, *This Dark Road to Mercy*, and *The Last Ballad*

"In *McMullen Circle*, Heather Newton's riveting novel in short story form, compelling and believably flawed characters inhabit Tonola Falls, Georgia, a small town on the cusp of integration. In a dozen connected stories, Newton weaves a tapestry of rich irony with fierce emotion and genuine bewilderment. Ordinary people, animated with astounding power, confront their weaknesses and principles in a baffling, rapidly changing world. Empathy and insight are forces as powerful as the stone mountain that supports and looms over these unforgettable stories."

—Anna Jean Mayhew, author of *The Dry Grass of August* and *Tomorrow's Bread*

"At turns dreamy and dark, Newton turns a deft eye toward the inhabitants of a small southern town on the cusp of turmoil—both in their inner lives and in the changing world around them—leaving the reader entranced."

—Kelly J. Ford, author of *Cottonmouths*

"Clear-sighted, restrained, deceptively simple, and eternally charitable, the stories that comprise *McMullen Circle* cohere deftly to create a devastating, life-affirming, vibrating, multi-voiced whole."

—Jen Fawkes, author of *Mannequin and Wife* and *Tales the Devil Told Me*

"Heather Newton is a beautiful writer and *McMullen Circle* is a beautiful book, written with compassion, humor and unflinching honesty. I love these stories, and as standalone pieces, each is compelling in its own way, often breathtakingly so. And read as a whole, the stories transcend the individual characters, offering a complex, conflicted and empathetic portrait of this North Georgia boarding school and its community. The whole time I was reading *McMullen Circle*, I was reminded again and again of Sherwood Anderson's *Winesburg, Ohio.* "

—Tommy Hays, author of *The Pleasure Was Mine*

"Heather Newton is a master at capturing the mood and longing of the late sixties, early seventies, and the isolation of a boarding school in the North Georgia mountains where the children run free and the headmaster's wife goes in search of a television. When the Cordelia Six are arrested for firebombing a nearby theater that wouldn't admit Black teenagers, the striations of race become wider and insistent. In this linked collection, the stories often turn on what is overheard or understood only by some or even on a simple gesture, and Newton's carefully crafted sentences place discovery and feeling squarely in the heart of the reader. *McMullen Circle* is forged out of our past, but this is a collection for now.

—Cynthia Newberry Martin, author of *Tidal Flats*

McMullen Circle

Heather Newton

Regal House Publishing

Published by
Regal House Publishing, LLC
Raleigh, NC 27612
All rights reserved

ISBN -13 (paperback): 9781646030767
ISBN -13 (epub): 9781646031016
Library of Congress Control Number: 2020948463

Interior and cover design by Lafayette & Greene
Cover images © by C. B. Royal

Regal House Publishing, LLC
https://regalhousepublishing.com

Printed in the United States of America

For Craig, Erin, and Michele

The mountain feels them walking on its surface. Their feet are part of its wearing down. Feet and wind and freeze and thaw and streams that carry its dust to the sea.

The mountain remembers the violence that came before the wearing down, when plates collided and seas opened and closed. Slivers of ocean floor still stripe its belly. It feels the ghostly ache of a piece ripped off and lodged to the south where the sun burns hot.

That age of tearing, of welding and suturing, is past. Now the mountain rests in a stillness which isn't still, but slow, invisibly slow, and it has time to watch and listen.

Wild Things

In some species of annuals, it is the parent plant that leaves the child, the dry stalks blowing away, leaving seeds in the soil.

—*Edible Wild Plants of North Georgia* by Simon Fisher

Prince Charles's investiture as the Prince of Wales would take place Tuesday, and Sarah had no place to watch it. All she wanted was a color television with decent reception, in the company of someone she could stand, to see Queen Elizabeth crown the young prince on the lawn of Caernarfon Castle. Their home didn't have a television because Sarah's husband, Richard, the headmaster of the McMullen Boarding School in Tonola Falls, Georgia, thought television rotted the brain.

Sarah walked along the circular paved road that ran in front of the school's administration building and ringed the campus. Faculty houses along the circle faced inward so teachers could monitor the dorms, but the students were on summer break and she was alone on the road. She had a book in her hand, *Edible Wild Plants of North Georgia*, but she wasn't reading it. She wanted to see the coronation, or investiture, whatever it was called. Sarah had been to Caernarfon Castle. When she was sixteen and in North Wales as an exchange student, she had leaned against the cold stone sill of one of the castle's tower windows, with a young man named Owen, the son of her host family, standing behind her with his arms around her waist. Light braided silver on the sea beyond the castle, and the grass was an impossible green in the courtyard below. She remembered the "Keep Off the Grass" signs in Welsh, *Peidiwch a mynd ar y borva*, as Owen traced the curve of her breasts with his thumbs. She had felt exotic and lovely then, something she didn't feel now, and she wanted to see that place again.

She reached her own house. Her daughter, Lorna, almost ten, was in the front yard showing her friend Chase Robbins how to do a back bend. Lorna wore purple nylon socks that Sarah hadn't been able to talk her out of that morning. When she bent backward her hair trailed the grass and her tie-dyed T-shirt came up, showing her ribs.

"I've got a job for you," Sarah said.

"We don't want a job," Chase said. Lorna struggled up from her back bend.

"A fun job," Sarah said. "I've got this book about wild plants you can eat. I thought you two could pick some dandelion greens for me. They're all over the backyard. You can pretend you're gathering food to survive in the wilderness."

That got Chase interested. "Well, okay," he said.

In the backyard Sarah showed them how to pick the newer greens, then went inside. She laid the edible plant book on the kitchen counter and looked out the window. Lorna and Chase had found a plastic flowerpot to collect the greens. They were at it in earnest, kneeling on the ground with Lorna's brown hair nearly touching Chase's red.

Sarah was having an affair with Chase's father, Art Robbins, the chemistry teacher. She had opened a flirtation with Art because no one else was available. She'd played him, reeling him in over a period of weeks with a skirt slit just so, hair tossed to release the smell of her shampoo. By the time she got him alone he was drooling. They screwed in the riskiest places she could find—once on the empty concrete bleachers of the football field at midnight, another time standing up against the tiled wall of the boys' locker room, with the smell of chlorine from the swimming pool stinging her nostrils. Art was nothing special. He mouth-breathed when they had sex and she could hardly bear to kiss him, but he served a need. He added an illusion of excitement for a while, and gave her something with which to hurt her husband Richard.

Lorna and Chase brought their full container of greens inside. Sarah put them in the sink to wash.

"Do you want to stay for lunch, Chase?"

Chase eyed the greens. "No, thanks," he said. "See you later."

Sarah heated up chicken noodle soup and fixed a salad with the dandelion greens. On top she shaved cucumber and radishes from a neighbor's garden and garnished it with nasturtium blossoms. It was really very pretty. When she heard Richard open the front door, she called Lorna to the table.

Richard walked into the kitchen and washed his hands at the sink. His had buttoned his white shirt at the sleeves and neck and fastened his tie with a McMullen School tiepin even though there were no students around to see him. She had once found that formality attractive, when she was a freshman at St. Mary's, a two-year women's college in Pennsylvania, and he was her professor. Now it was hard to remember why.

She put the soup on the table and broached the subject of a television. "I was wondering if we might rent a color TV, just for a day, so I can watch them crown the Prince of Wales."

"It wouldn't work," Richard said. "The reception's so bad up here. You'd need an outside antenna."

"I suppose you're right." Stone encased the school campus, the buildings and walls blending into the mountain behind them. Without an antenna, installed with arms outstretched in a *T* on the roof of the house, airwaves couldn't get through.

Richard and Lorna sat down to eat. Sarah put the dandelion salad in the middle of the table.

"What's that?" Richard said.

"Wild dandelion green salad, from a book I picked up at the health food store. I thought we could try something new."

Lorna picked a leaf out of the bowl and tasted the tip.

"How is it?" Sarah said.

"Okay," Lorna said loyally. "A little fuzzy."

Richard reached over and lifted some salad onto his plate. The greens were tough and he chewed for a long time.

"It's a bit late in the season," Sarah said. "They'd be more tender right when they come out."

He got up and went to the refrigerator, took out a head of

iceberg lettuce and a bottle of Thousand Island dressing, and sat back down.

Lorna looked at Sarah.

"You don't have to finish it," Sarah said.

All the girls in Sarah's college dorm thought the new English professor was handsome. Richard Pierce was tall and serious, his hair already receding in his late twenties, with a way of listening attentively to even the silliest young women in his class. Sarah found him far more interesting than the boys who drove over from the coed college across the river for group dates on Saturday nights.

"He's so distinguished," breathed her suite mate, Mitzi.

Of the four girls in their suite, Sarah intended to be the one to win the young professor's attention—not plain Mitzi of the books and unshaped eyebrows, or icy Charlotte who was saving herself for marriage. And Richard was too solemn for Babs.

She started by loosening her top button so that her blouse opened to a shadow of breast when he stood over her handing back a paper. She could tell he noticed by the extra seconds he let pass before he moved on to the next student. She met his eyes as he lectured, causing him to fumble and drop his chalk. She rested her pencil eraser on her lower lip and smoothed her hair behind her ear just so. She stayed after class pretending to need help deciphering his written comments on her essay. Her upper arm touched his as he translated. He didn't move away. When she was sure she had him she went searching the dim halls of the humanities building until she found his office.

He was at his desk, reading. When he saw her, his index finger froze above the page. She stepped inside and closed the door behind her.

He cleared his throat. "Did you need something?"

She went around to his side of the desk and stood with her legs between his knees. For a moment she thought he would try to pretend not to know why she was there, but he placed his hands on her waist and rested his forehead against her stomach, closing his eyes. She stripped for him, out of the starch and itch of her blouse and wool skirt. Richard unbuttoned his shirt, undid his belt. His mouth was over hers, his hands rough and warm on her skin. Books and papers slid to the floor and Richard breathed a sigh in her ear that sounded like he had been holding his breath forever.

She went to his office most afternoons after class and met him at a motel off campus on the weekends, away from his nosy landlord. The sex was delicious and so were the debriefings in the dorm afterward—her suite mates in bathrobes and towel turbans, hungry for every luscious detail. Mitzi falling back on the bed hugging her pillow as Sarah described making love in Richard's office while the department chair chatted in the corridor.

Only once did Richard speak of ending it, as they lay naked on the floor in front of his desk. "We have to stop this. Other students suspect. They're claiming favoritism."

She ran her palm slowly along the hollow between his navel and the ridge of his pelvic bone. His breath caught in his throat.

"Go ahead and flunk me," she said.

In the late afternoon Sarah walked over to the stone patio in front of the McMullen School's administration building, where the younger faculty couples held happy hour when the students were on break. From the patio they could look down on their children playing on the broad, sloping lawn below. Shade from tall hemlocks kept them relatively cool. Richard allowed it even though he didn't come, afraid it might erode his already tenuous authority. Sarah was a regular.

Art Robbins had pulled a blue plastic baby pool up onto the patio and hosed it full of water. Art and his wife Patsy, Catherine Mayhew, and Sarah pulled their lawn chairs close so they could put their feet in. Catherine, whose husband Greg taught math, was seven months pregnant. She tucked her short blond hair behind her ears and swished her feet in the water. "This feels so damn good." Across from Sarah, Patsy Robbins sat stiffly in her chair next to Art. Patsy and Art were mismatched, though not as much as Art liked to think. Patsy didn't have a college education like he did. They'd married when Patsy was seventeen and got pregnant with their daughter Mandy. Patsy was one step out of the western North Carolina coves and Art made fun of her, though he was only a generation from Georgia dirt himself and not as worldly or interesting as he thought he was.

Sarah looked at all of their bare feet in the water and decided hers were the best. They were slender, tanned on top but pale between the toes, and she had painted her nails a pearl pink. Catherine's feet were cute but her ankles were swollen. Patsy's were pedicured but stumpy, the toes too short. Art's feet looked terrible, the toenails yellowed by some fungus, calluses on the heels. Sarah lifted her right foot out of the water to better admire it and saw Art staring at it. She pointed her toes at him slightly and gave him an amused smile. Patsy saw, and took her feet out of the pool, crossing her legs away from Art.

Art had brought a cooler of beer and a big bottle of cheap gin for gin and tonics. He poured their drinks. Catherine couldn't partake because she was pregnant. "Give me a goddamned tonic water," she said, not really sounding perturbed. Catherine's husband Greg was down on the lawn, running around with the kids, his lanky body stretching as he chased them. Greg would have been Sarah's first choice for an affair, but he was ridiculously in love with his wife.

Art handed Sarah and Patsy gin and tonics in plastic cups. Patsy got out her cigarettes and Art held out his hand for one.

"I'll give you one if you'll actually smoke it," Patsy said. "I hate when you light it and just hold it up letting it burn."

"Just pass me the cigarette," Art said.

"What I wouldn't give for a smoke," Catherine said. "Two more months."

Sarah sipped her drink. Down on the lawn Greg Mayhew had lined the kids up in front of the chapel, where the chapel bell had its own open-sided shelter about eight feet tall. He had tied a plastic jump rope to the bell's regular rope so the smallest kids could reach. Each kid got a turn ringing the bell. Lorna was in line in front of Chase, dancing from one foot to the other. When it was her turn, instead of ringing the bell herself, she handed the rope to Chase and ran under the bell so she could see what the clapper mechanism looked like when he rang it. "Pull harder!" she called. She was a little scientist, always taking the backs off things, wanting to know how they worked. Sarah loved her daughter with a fierceness that sometimes terrified her, but she didn't always understand her.

Sarah turned back to happy hour. "Is anyone planning to watch the Prince of Wales on Tuesday?"

"I wouldn't miss it," Patsy said. "It's so exciting. I remember when they crowned Queen Elizabeth. And when she got engaged. My aunt was making toast when she heard the news. She mailed the toast to Princess Elizabeth for a wedding gift."

Art snorted. "Why are American women so obsessed with monarchy?"

Patsy ignored him. "I always thought I'd marry a prince."

"Where were you going to meet him? The Hicksville polo club?" Art said.

Patsy took a drag on her cigarette. The corners of her mouth sagged. "Well, I sure as hell didn't marry one," she said.

Art could smirk at Patsy for thinking she would marry a prince, but Sarah, too, had imagined she'd marry a prince. Not Prince Charles, who was nine years younger than she, but there were other princes. Grace Kelly had found one. There were all manner of minor kingdoms out there—Liechtenstein, Saxe-Coburg and Gotha. She would have made a good princess. Instead she'd married Richard.

Her toes were shriveling. She took her feet out of the water. "I need someone with a color TV to invite me over to watch it," she said.

"All we've got is black and white, and it rolls so badly it'll make you nauseous," Catherine said.

"Watch it at our place," Art said.

Patsy glared at him. "We might not be here. I'm thinking of taking the kids to my mother's."

"I'll be here," Art said.

Patsy's face pinked. Sarah knew Patsy suspected the affair. Sarah reveled in it, goading Patsy when she got the chance. She couldn't help it, though she always felt bad afterward.

She looked out at the children playing on the school lawn, which sloped steeply down to a retaining wall at the bottom. The children were running down the hill full speed and then leaping off the wall, a good five-foot drop. Lorna's long brown hair flew out behind her as she ran. Lorna reached the wall and sailed off, suspended in air long enough for Sarah to imagine a hundred bad landings, a hundred ways she could lose her child, before Lorna landed expertly in a crouch and ran around the wall and up the hill to do it again.

Sarah turned back to the circle around the pool and gave Patsy a sweet smile. "I'll think about your invitation," she said, to watch Patsy squirm. She finished the last of her drink and tipped her ice cubes into the pool. It was entertaining to panic Patsy Robbins, but it left Sarah bereft. She had no friend to watch a damn television event with.

The next day Sarah had promised to take Lorna to the county fair. She walked over to Richard's office in the administration building to get the checkbook. When she got there, Mrs. Dolores Vaughan Parke, president emeritus of the Atlanta Women's Club that had founded the McMullen School, sat in the chair opposite Richard. Mrs. Parke was in her eighties. Her father had donated the land for the school and she still exercised a proprietary interest, driving up, unannounced, on a regular basis to complain to Richard about one thing or another. Richard's left eyelid flicked with the strain of dealing with her.

"Excuse me," Sarah said. "I didn't know you were in with Mrs. Parke."

"Don't apologize, dear," said Mrs. Parke. "We were just finishing up some Board business." With effort, she turned her stooped body toward Sarah. "Richard tells me you're looking for a place to watch the investiture. You can watch it at the hotel with me. I once met the queen, you know. Or almost. Mr. Parke and I attended a garden party at Windsor Castle. We were twenty people away from her in the receiving line and it started to rain. They bustled her away."

Sarah didn't want to watch the investiture with Mrs. Parke. She could have killed Richard for mentioning it to her.

"They won't be photographed eating, you know, the royal family," Mrs. Parke said.

"Oh? Afraid of being caught with spinach in their teeth?" Sarah said, and watched Richard's face flush. "Thank you for offering, Mrs. Parke, but I've made other plans."

"Suit yourself," Mrs. Parke said.

"Richard, I need the checkbook," Sarah said.

"What for?" he said.

"The fair." She challenged him to ask her any more questions in front of Mrs. Parke. He scrutinized every penny she spent, making her get his approval in advance. To spite him she had started writing checks at the grocery store for five dollars over, squirreling the money away in her lingerie drawer where she knew he would never look.

Richard glanced at Mrs. Parke, then reached in his desk and handed Sarah the checkbook. "Lovely seeing you, Mrs. Parke," Sarah said, and stepped out the door.

Sarah's affair with Richard had cost him his position at St. Mary's, even though she dropped his class and they got married at the courthouse before the end of the school year to legitimize the relationship. It was too awkward for the administration to handle—if he'd gotten involved with one student, what was to stop him from doing it again? The college gave him a good reference to help him move on.

The day after finals ended Sarah stood on the curb while Mitzi, Charlotte, and Babs loaded the last of their belongings into Charlotte's convertible. The girls were headed to the Jersey Shore where Charlotte's grandparents owned a house.

"I can't believe you're not coming with us," Mitzi said, giving

Sarah a hug. Mitzi smelled of the lemon juice she'd used to streak her hair so it would lighten in the summer sun.

"I'm a married lady now." Sarah flashed her gold wedding band.

Mitzi barely looked at the ring. "You'll keep in touch, won't you, honey?" Concern creased the corners of her eyes.

"All aboard," Charlotte called.

Sarah accepted perfumed goodbyes from Charlotte and Babs and helped Mitzi stash a box of books under the front seat. She waved as her friends pulled away.

"Whoo-hoooo!" Babs whipped her navy-blue St. Mary's cardigan in a circle above her head and let go. The sweater flew into the road and the convertible disappeared around a curve. Sarah turned to find Richard standing in front of the dorm, his arms crossed in disapproval. She stepped out into the road and retrieved Babs's sweater before joining him to pack up her own things.

Once Sarah's girlfriends weren't around to admire her seducing the professor, it wasn't so fun anymore.

Sarah and Lorna arrived at the fair early, before it got too hot. They walked down the midway. Lorna had brought her own money, dollar bills stuffed into a denim change purse with butterflies embroidered on it. There were two things Lorna liked to do at the fair that Sarah wouldn't give her money for because she didn't approve. One was a rip-off dart game where the darts bounced off balloons instead of popping them. The other was the freak show. Freaks fascinated Lorna: the world's largest horse, the world's smallest goat, two-headed sheep. The freak show was housed behind a tall canvas fence that ran in a ribboned maze, blocking the view of anyone who hadn't paid admission. Elaborate posters outside promised sightings of Mermaid Girl, Bird Boy, the Devil's Son.

"I'm not paying two dollars for that. It's not a good use of money," Sarah said.

Lorna shrugged and handed two dollars to the carnie at the

entrance. She entered the canvas maze. For a moment Sarah could see the shadow of her feet through the small gap in the bottom of the fence, then Lorna disappeared from view.

The sun hung overhead now, and it was starting to get hot. Sarah watched a man at a concession stand across the way pour a squiggle of dough into his deep fryer. Behind his booth a Ferris wheel rose, full of screaming children. Beside the freak show a teenaged boy managed to pop enough balloons in the dart game to win his girlfriend a stuffed bear. Sarah wiped sweat from her upper lip.

A child who had gone in to see the freaks behind Lorna emerged from the maze. Sarah felt her heart freeze. Lorna had been in there too long. Who knew what these carnies were up to? Someone could have snatched her and taken her out the back without Sarah seeing. Panic rose in her throat. Another child emerged. Sarah started for the entrance, ready to bully her way past the man taking money, and Lorna walked calmly out of the maze.

Sarah took a deep breath and let it out. "How was it?"

"Good."

"Worth two dollars?"

"Oh yeah."

"What was it like?"

"Well, the Devil's Child and Mermaid Girl were just dolls with a bunch of dirt on them, they weren't alive. Bird Boy too."

"Not like the posters?

"No." Lorna didn't sound disappointed. "They said Mermaid Girl washed up on a beach and that's how they found her."

"Were any of them alive?"

"Most of them were just pickled, like the Cyclops Pig, but the six-legged cow was alive."

"And it was really worth the money?" Sarah said.

Lorna gave a happy little jump. "I loved it. Next year will you come in with me?"

"Yes." Sarah rested a hand on the top of Lorna's head, and steered her up the midway. She could not live without this child. She had been to see a lawyer in Clayton, who stared at her breasts the entire consultation and had no hope to offer. If she left Richard he would fight for custody, and in this part of Georgia, fathers always won. She would have to lie to him, tell him she was taking Lorna to visit her parents in Pennsylvania, and just not come back. But then how would she support the two of them? Sarah didn't have a college degree. Before her abbreviated stint at Saint Mary's she had done a course at modeling school. Charm school, really. She learned poses, posture, and poise. She learned how, before sitting down in a chair, to slide her left foot over, parallel with her right, press her knees together prettily and then sit, an amazing skill that had captivated men ever since but wouldn't transfer to the workplace. She didn't do the foot slide for Richard anymore. She had considered teaching it to Lorna, but Lorna was made of more substance than that. Sarah could imagine Lorna's response, her questions about why she needed to learn to sit down that way.

"Will you come in the House of Mirrors with me?" Lorna said.

"Yes," Sarah said, not wanting to let Lorna out of her sight again.

In the House of Mirrors, where all the mirrors were fogged with the greasy handprints of groping children, Sarah saw something and leaned closer to get a better look. It was a single gray hair, bending coarse above the brown on the right side of her head, refusing to lie down. She twined it around two fingers and yanked it out, angrily shaking it off her fingers so it floated to the floor.

With the edible plant book in hand, Sarah wandered outside to the stone patio behind her house. All along the waist-high stone wall that separated patio from mountain, daylilies grew, some planted by the previous headmaster, some she'd planted herself. They were just budding, some partially opened. With her kitchen scissors she gathered the buds, snipping them cleanly the way the book instructed, each bud making a pinging sound as she dropped it into the metal bowl.

Back inside she heated a sauté pan and watched the butter melt, then stir-fried the buds. She tried one. It tasted like asparagus, only wilder somehow. The clean-air smell around the bud's edges pleased her, and as she heard Richard open the front door, she tipped the buds into a white china bowl that would set off their bright orangy-green color. Lorna came in and sat down and Richard followed. Sarah brought the meal to the table, proudly setting the bowl of daylily buds down in the middle.

"What are those?" Richard said.

"Daylily buds. They taste exactly like asparagus," Sarah said.

Lorna spooned a bud out on to her plate and tried it. "It's good. Buttery." She ladled a few more onto her plate.

Richard stood up and went to the back door, looking out. "Sarah. You cut off all the buds. You didn't leave any."

"I needed enough for a meal," she said.

Richard turned to face them. "Lorna, where do daylily flowers come from?"

"From buds," Lorna said, pulling the tough end of a bud out of her mouth.

Richard looked at Sarah. "You've destroyed the daylilies. We won't have any flowers this year."

"Just eat the goddamned meal I prepared," Sarah said, but she knew he was right. She cut up a bud and put it in her mouth. It was stringy on her tongue. She had exterminated her favorite flowers.

The day of the investiture, Richard went into Clayton and bought more daylilies. He and Lorna worked together in the backyard, planting them intermittently among the ones Sarah had decapitated. Sarah watched through the screen door as Richard showed Lorna how to divide the roots of a particularly thick cluster. There was something tender in the way his body bowed slightly over hers, his normal stiffness and reserve put away. Lorna held the plant's bulb up close to her face to examine it.

Sarah had finally figured out a place to watch Prince Charles be crowned, remembering the televisions in the school's classrooms. She stepped out onto the back steps. "Lorna, the coronation is in ten minutes." She said it tentatively, afraid Lorna would turn her down so she could continue planting with Richard. Lorna looked up at Richard.

"It's okay, we're at a good stopping place," he said.

Lorna ran past Sarah into the house to wash up.

Richard stood looking at Sarah, his dirty hands hanging at his sides. He started to say something, then closed his mouth and shook his head slightly, turning away.

Sarah and Lorna walked over to the main school building. It was built into the rock, keeping the empty classrooms cool. Lorna helped Sarah pull an audiovisual cart out of a closet and plug the television in. They sat down at desks. Sarah's knees pressed against the underside of the desktop.

They watched the processional of guardsmen in red uniforms and brushy hats. The lawn of Caernarfon Castle was as green as Sarah remembered, and there was Queen Elizabeth all alone in a chair on a low circular stage at its center, waiting for her son. The queen's short yellow dress matched her hat. She pressed her pudgy knees together. The camera panned for a moment, turning toward the castle towers. Sarah scanned the tower windows for the one where she had once stood. She wanted to see movement, a girl's hand resting on the ledge, but the windows were gaping black holes. The camera returned to queen and prince. The prince, looking too young for the huge crown on his head, took his mother's hands and began to speak. Microphones picked up the sound of wind from the sea blowing around his voice.

I, Charles, Prince of Wales, do become your liege man of life and limb and of earthly worship, and faith and truth I will bear unto you to live and die against all manner of folks.

"What's that mean?" Lorna said.

"Nothing," Sarah said. "It's nonsense."

Back at the house she fixed Lorna a pimiento cheese sandwich and sent her outside to eat it on the steps. Through the screen she could hear Lorna singing "Hey Jude," her voice endearingly off key. Sarah went and leaned against the door frame, looking at the back of Lorna's head. She tested a thought in her mind, of walking out the door, up the road, onto the highway heading north. If she left quickly perhaps it wouldn't hurt any more than the pulling off of a Band-Aid. But she couldn't do it, not yet, and she pushed through the screen door to join Lorna on the steps.

McMullen Circle

Chase Robbins and Lorna Pierce sat on the curb in the July heat, watching the family across the street move out. A glorious junk pile grew in front of their house. Chase had already spotted a flaking decoy duck and an almost-full box of military C-rations left over from World War II, twenty-five years before. If the Sandersons would hurry up and leave, Chase and Lorna could root through the pile and get the best stuff before anybody else showed up. Whenever a family moved, there was never anything left for the garbage men to pick up. It all went home in pieces with the neighborhood kids, to show up again on future junk piles when other families left. A lot of families left. The McMullen School in Tonola Falls, Georgia, owned the circle of faculty houses where Chase and Lorna lived. The boarding school was prestigious but didn't pay much, and teachers moved away during the summer if they got a better offer.

The noon air raid siren from the Tonola Falls fire department wailed in the still air. Chase scratched the heads off his mosquito bites. Lorna examined the dots the cement curb had pressed into the backs of her thighs. Mr. and Mrs. Sanderson and their daughter Mary came out of the front door of their house and locked it for the last time. Mary was ten, a year older than Lorna and two years older than Chase. She was a little goofy. She waved at Chase and Lorna across the yard. "Bye, y'all!"

They waved back. "Bye, Mary."

Mrs. Sanderson and Mary got into the family's navy-blue Plymouth Belvedere and drove off. Mr. Sanderson climbed into the cab of the moving van with the moving men. The truck backed up into the street. Chase and Lorna stood up and got out of its way. Finally the truck moved forward, down the street and out of sight, and Chase and Lorna ran for the junk pile.

Chase lugged the cardboard box of C-rations from the top of the pile. The bottom of the box fell out and cans dropped and rolled. Chase picked up one of the bigger ones and read the words stamped on it. "Corned beef hash." He held it up so Lorna could see it from where she dug. "There's a little can opener with it." He rooted through the rest of the C-rations, using his corner teeth to open a rectangular packet. Inside were salt and pepper and a tiny square of toilet paper. He was trying to get the wrapper off a roll of fused Life Savers when Lorna called to him from the other side of the heap.

"Look." She held up a perfectly good plastic Halloween pumpkin, the kind for collecting treats.

"Is there any candy in it?" Chase dropped the expired Life Savers on the ground and went over to see.

Lorna shook it. "No."

Chase examined the pumpkin. Its black strap wasn't even broken. He wished he had found it.

"Hey," Lorna said. "I have an idea."

Lorna had good ideas. One time she started a store and sold all her old junk to some stupid little kids, until their mother came around the circle to complain and Lorna's mom made her give their money back. Another time she and Chase set a trap for the neighborhood bully, Duncan McAfee, otherwise known as Duncan Donut. They climbed a tree where they thought he might pass by, tied a plastic jump rope around a brick, and waited for Duncan so they could drop the brick on him. It was exciting even though Duncan Donut never showed up.

"Let's go trick-or-treating," Lorna said.

"It's not Halloween."

"A lot of people have candy even when it's not Halloween." Lorna's eyes glinted. Her dad, the school's headmaster, hardly ever let her have candy.

"Do we have to wear a costume?"

"No, too hot."

"Okay, but I'm taking my stuff home first." Chase picked up the decoy duck and found a box with a bottom for his C-rations.

Lorna hadn't found anything else that interested her as much as the pumpkin.

The Atlanta Women's Club had started the McMullen School so city kids could breathe fresh Georgia mountain air. The school boarded high school students but provided a small lower school for the children of faculty like Chase and Lorna, so they wouldn't have to go all the way to Clarksville to public school. The school's buildings were made from stone quarried out of the mountain. A high rock wall behind the administration building held back the mountain. The school had expelled high school boys for climbing the wall to impress their girlfriends, risking the three-story fall. The calves of Chase and Lorna's legs were hard as stone from climbing all over the hilly campus.

Chase and Lorna walked around the circle of faculty houses to Chase's, where they could hear his mom yelling even before they got inside. She yelled a lot. Sometimes she waited for Chase to go into the next room just so she could yell for him instead of speaking in a normal voice. Today she was yelling at somebody else. Chase's big sister Mandy and her boyfriend, Wally, sat at the Formica table in the kitchen, drinking Cokes. Chase's mom yelled from the living room. "I told him I wanted these screens put back in today!" She banged the living room windows shut. "The mosquitos are eating us alive. He thinks his work ends when school's out and he doesn't have papers to grade. My work doesn't end, why should his?"

Mandy winked at Chase, trying not to laugh. Wally, always polite, tried to look serious.

"I told you, I don't know where Dad went," Mandy called. She played with Wally's big class ring on her pointer finger.

Chase snuck down the hall and put his junk pile treasures in his bedroom, then came back out to the kitchen. Lorna, who spent as much time at Chase's house as she did at hers, sat at the table with Mandy and Wally. Chase's mom came in from the living room and leaned in the kitchen doorway. The hair she had sprayed into place so carefully that morning draggled around her sweaty face. "Chase, where is your father?"

"I don't know."

His mom heaved a sigh. She left the room muttering, "I'm going to kill him. I'm just going to kill him."

Mandy smiled at Chase and Lorna. "Did the Sandersons leave anything good?" At seventeen, she was too grown up to go digging in junk piles herself, but she appreciated a good find. One time Chase found her a half-full bottle of Chanel No. 5, which she still wore. Mandy always smelled good.

"We got this." Lorna put her plastic pumpkin on the table.

Wally thumped the pumpkin. "That'll come in handy come fall."

"We're going to use it today," Lorna said. "Trick or treat!"

Chase chimed in, "Trick or treat! We're going to take it around the neighborhood and see if we get any candy."

Mandy and Wally laughed. "You two are crazy," Mandy said.

"I think it's a great idea." Wally reached in his jeans pocket. "Lemme see what I got." He looked through the stuff in his palm. He picked out two quarters and two pieces of Dentyne and dropped them in the pumpkin.

"Gee, thanks!" Chase was happy to see that summer trick-or-treating really worked.

"Where you headed next?" Wally said.

They really hadn't thought about it.

"You ought to try the old ladies," Mandy said. "They'll give you something." It was a good idea.

The old ladies were loud Miss Evelyn, the school librarian, and her sweet friend, Miss Margaret. Miss Evelyn had a deep voice that carried even when she whispered in the library. She had published a novel back in the 1920s that was racy enough that Chase's mom wouldn't let Mandy read it. Miss Margaret had come to the school with Miss Evelyn. She used to be a professional singer, until her voice got too wobbly. Now she directed the school's chapel choir every Sunday. Sometimes if Miss Margaret wanted you to speak up, she would do her arms like a conductor trying to pull more sound out of the violin section.

When Chase and Lorna knocked on the ladies' door, Miss Margaret answered. She had bright red hair with an inch of white roots, and orange lipstick.

"Trick or treat!" Chase and Lorna had practiced saying it together.

Miss Margaret's hands flew up in the air. "My goodness, aren't you two clever. Come inside while I look and see what we have."

They followed her down the dark hall, into the ladies' living room. "Have a seat." They sat down on a hard sofa with scratchy green upholstery and elegant legs. The room smelled like old lady, rose powder and things shut up in boxes too long. Miss Evelyn went to a cut-glass jar on an end table and took the lid off. The jar was a third of the way full of old-fashioned ribbon candy. Miss Evelyn turned the jar upside down. The candy was so old it stuck to the bottom and wouldn't come out. "Oh dear," she said.

"I can get it!" Chase scooted off the sofa and took the jar from her.

"Now be careful, dear, that jar belonged to Evelyn's mother."

Chase stuck his hand all the way into the jar and scraped with his fingertips. Some corners of the ribbon candy broke off, then the whole congealed wad came out at once. He held it up, triumphant. "Can we have the whole thing?"

"Of course you can." Miss Margaret beamed. "We can't eat hard candy. It sticks to our teeth."

They heard the front door open, and Miss Evelyn's deep voice as she came down the hall. "You'll never guess who I saw swimming together in the gym pool, Margaret." She entered the living room and stopped when she saw Chase and Lorna.

Miss Margaret held her left hand still in the air and wafted her fingers at Miss Evelyn, the way Arthur Fiedler did on the Boston Pops when he wanted to tone down the trombones. "The children are here trick-or-treating, Evelyn."

"Who was swimming in the pool?" Lorna asked. The pool was off limits during the summer.

Miss Evelyn ran a hand through her short gray hair. "Nobody." She grabbed the rim of Lorna's pumpkin and peered inside. "That all you got?"

"So far," Chase said.

"Well, here." Miss Evelyn strode off to the kitchen and came back with two Moon Pies. "They're big, anyway. Make you feel like you have something in there." She dropped them into the pumpkin with a thunk.

"Thanks, Miss Evelyn." Moon Pies were Chase's favorite.

"And thank you, Miss Margaret," Lorna said.

Lorna lived two doors down from the old ladies. Her dad, Mr. Pierce, the headmaster, was out in the front yard, trimming his rose bushes. His long-sleeved white shirt was buttoned at the wrists, and sweat made his undershirt show through it. His scalp was starting to sunburn through his thin hair. Mr. Pierce was a lot older than Lorna's mother, and a lot less interesting. Mrs. Pierce had been one of Mr. Pierce's students. Chase's dad didn't like Mr. Pierce, maybe because the headmaster never laughed at his jokes. Chase liked him okay.

They stopped in front of him, to be polite. "Hi, Mr. Pierce," Chase said.

"Hello, Chase. Hello, Lorna." Mr. Pierce wasn't really paying attention to them. He clipped a dead branch off a yellow rose bush.

Chase and Lorna looked at each other. "Well, see you later, Dad," Lorna said.

Mr. Pierce's lifted his head and peered at them over his wire-framed glasses. "What are you two up to?"

Lorna swung the plastic pumpkin. "We're just trick-or-treating. Pretending."

Mr. Pierce closed his clippers. "You aren't bothering anybody, I hope."

"No, Dad."

He turned back to his pruning. "See that you don't."

"We won't." Lorna looked around. "Is Mom here?"

"No. I don't know where she is."

If Mrs. Pierce wasn't in, there was no point looking for treats inside Lorna's house. Chase and Lorna continued around the circle.

The next occupied house was the McAfees'. Duncan Donut McAfee was away at camp for the summer, terrorizing a new set of kids, so Chase rang the doorbell. As soon as he rang, he knew they had made a mistake.

Mrs. McAfee answered the door. Mrs. McAfee was religious. Once when Chase accidentally ran over the irises in her side yard with his bicycle, she told him he was going to hell. Chase rode home and told his dad, who sent him back to Mrs. McAfee to tell her there was no such thing as hell. "You tell your dad yes there is, and he's going there too," Mrs. McAfee had said.

Mrs. McAfee crossed her fat arms. "Does your father know what you're up to, Lorna? And you ought to be ashamed, Chase Robbins. Your mother has enough to worry about without her child begging the neighbors for candy." Then her face went from mean to sweet and she changed her voice to the tone people use when they deliver a casserole after a funeral. "Tell your poor mother that if she needs anything, anything at all, she should just call me."

Chase couldn't see telling his mom to call on Mrs. McAfee for anything, when he and Lorna hadn't been able to squeeze so much as a raisin out of the woman. "Yes, ma'am," he said. Mrs. McAfee closed her door.

Chase was hot and hungry. "Let's sit down and eat those Moon Pies."

"No," Lorna said. "It'll be better if we dump it all out in a big pile at the end of the day."

Chase gave in. Lorna was smarter than him. "Hey, we ought to try the Victory Home," he said. The home for men with drinking problems was only a half-mile from the school. Chase went there a lot. The men had nothing to do but sit on the front porch and whittle. Thanks to them, Chase had the largest collection of slingshots around.

When they got to the Victory Home, Chase's friend Danny was on the porch. Chase's dad said Danny drank because he'd had a bad war. Danny was thin, his hair gray on the sides. His hands shook when he carved slingshots for Chase or lit a cigarette. Other men came and went, but Danny lived at the home for good.

Danny sat in the wide swing at the end of the Victory Home porch. He saw Chase and Lorna and waved. "What you got there, a jack-o'-lantern?"

They walked up the steps and sat down in white rocking chairs near the swing. Their feet dangled. Chase leaned way forward then back again to get rocking. "We're trick-or-treating," he said.

"What month is it?" For a minute Danny looked worried, like it might be October and he had lost the time between.

"July," Chase said. "We found the pumpkin on the Sandersons' move-out pile."

"They gone already?" Danny fumbled with the cord of the bathrobe he wore, to tighten it. "Seems like somebody's always moving out over there, for one reason or another. Your daddy can't seem to hold on to his teachers, Lorna."

"They leave for better opportunities." Lorna sounded like the headmaster.

Danny eyed their pumpkin. "I got something for you, I think. Wait right here." He stood and walked slowly into the big house. His bedroom slippers made scuffing sounds on the porch boards. When he came back a minute later, he had a canister of butterscotch candy that had never been opened. He sat back down in the swing and worked the top off. "My sister sent me this. Don't care for it, myself." His hands shook as he poured the whole can into the pumpkin, filling it to the brim.

"Wow," Chase said.

"Thanks, Danny," Lorna said.

"You're welcome. Come back again, she sends me some about every week."

They left the Victory Home and walked back to Lorna's house. Her dad wasn't in the front yard. "Let's go dump it all out," Lorna said. They went around to the brick patio the last headmaster had built to make use of the tiny strip of backyard the mountain allowed before it rose behind the house. The sun blinded Chase for a second as they rounded the corner. He saw people moving and heard a metal chair scrape on brick. His dad and Lorna's mom sat at a glass-topped table under a sun umbrella, drinking iced tea. Mint leaves hung over the sides of their Tupperware drinking glasses.

Lorna had the prettiest mother in the neighborhood. She wore a white blouse with flowy sleeves and a denim skirt with a slit up the side that showed one long leg. Her dark brown hair was slicked back, but usually fell thick around her face. She had a habit of reaching over her head with one hand to pull the hair away from the other side of her face. Chase's mom talked bad about Lorna's mom because Mrs. Pierce was a feminist, and because she went to the Unitarian church in Clarksville even though the headmaster expected all the other teachers and their families to attend chapel on campus. Chase thought Mrs. Pierce was beautiful.

Chase's dad turned toward them and crossed a leg. He had almost no hair on his crew-cut head, but he had hairy legs. "Here comes trouble," he said.

"Hi, sweetie." Mrs. Pierce reached an arm for Lorna and hugged her around the waist. She scooted her chair around the table away from Chase's dad and pulled another chair up beside her. "Want to sit?"

Lorna stayed standing and brought out the pumpkin. She poured their stuff onto the glass tabletop. It looked magnificent. "We got it trick-or-treating," she said.

Chase's dad poked a finger through the candy. "Not a bad off-season haul."

"You can have a piece," Chase said. "But not the Moon Pie."

"Thanks, sport."

"Hey, Dad, Mom was looking for you."

Chase's dad pulled his hand back from the candy pile and looked at Mrs. Pierce.

She turned away from him. "I guess I need to get dinner ready soon."

Chase's dad stood up. He ducked his head so he wouldn't hit it on the sun umbrella. "Come on, sport."

Mrs. Pierce drew her leg up and examined her perfect toenails. Lorna divided up the candy. Since she got to keep the pumpkin, Chase stuffed his share into his pockets.

"Maybe we can do it again next week," he said.

"Maybe." Lorna seemed to have lost interest.

Chase and his dad stepped off the patio and walked toward home. Chase offered his dad the piece of Dentyne that Wally had given him.

"Hang on a second." Chase's dad tilted his head down to his left shoulder and bounced on his left foot, a finger in his left ear.

Chase looked back. Lorna stood behind her mother's chair, her forehead crinkled like she was trying to figure something out, braiding her mother's damp hair.

Tupelo Rose

Danny remembered the river, the way it curved like a thick snake under them, moonlight glinting off its scales, thick foliage rising up from both banks. The non-sound of the plane's missing engine, taken out by flak, its voice no longer screaming with the other three. A chunk the size of a tire bitten off the tail. From the tail gun, Danny could see the hole. The hard yaw as Burton, the pilot, fought to hold her steady. Intercom silent as they all listened. Parachutes ready. Sweat on Sweeney's face a few feet away, despite the freezing cold.

It was the river he always remembered first, before the bad stuff that followed. The way it gained texture and color as the plane lost altitude. He saw the *S* of that river in everything. The swirling paisley on Matron's skirt when she brought him his iced tea on the porch. The rubber bands the other Victory Home residents used for the slingshots they whittled. The red streak of enemy flare when the Germans spotted them, as Danny hacked at Sweeney's parachute, trying to cut him loose from the tree. Sweeney's intestines swinging from a German soldier's bayonet while Sweeney screamed. The swayed back of the emaciated man Danny saw reflected in metal the day the allies liberated the prison camp, before he realized the reflection was his. Nearly thirty years of *S* shapes since the war. Not one day free. Some better now because he wasn't drinking anymore. Some worse, because he wasn't drinking anymore.

Danny sat in his usual spot on the porch swing at the Victory Home, a residential facility for men with drinking problems. Other men stayed a month, but Danny had been here for two years, some special dispensation Matron had arranged with the Board, without which he'd be dead by now. It was ten o'clock in the morning. Sun had already burned off the dew. Insects trilled in the grass in front of the home. The heavy smell of

Ligustrum blossoms from the bush behind Danny made it hard to breathe.

The town of Tonola Falls, up the road, had a post office, a municipal building that was really a garage for the town's one police car and fire truck, and not much else, except a private boarding school, the McMullen School, which perched on a hill looking down on the town. Along the road from town came Danny's buddy Chase Robbins, an eight-year-old whose father taught at the school. He had a stick in his hand and whacked the Queen Anne's lace that grew along the road. Chase reached the Victory Home porch and tossed his stick down before joining Danny on the swing. His legs weren't long enough to reach the porch boards. Band-Aids covered scabs on both knees.

Danny looked down at Chase's buzz-cut hair and freckled nose. "You're early," he said. "Afraid you'd miss something?"

"My mom told me get out of the house," Chase said.

Matron stepped onto the porch, her sensible shoes silent, salt and pepper hair curled respectably over her ears. "You doing all right out here, Danny?"

"Yes, ma'am."

"Colonel Burton will be here soon." She went back inside.

Colonel Mackie Burton, USAF, Retired, the pilot Danny flew with in the war, was coming here today, to the Victory Home. Burton, the pilot of the *Tupelo Rose*.

"Boys, I can fly her, but I can't turn her around," Burton's voice had come over the intercom that night. "I say we bail now, before Germany."

"Where we at, Cap'n?" Sweeney said.

"Belgium."

One by one they bailed, Burton at the yoke. Danny waited for Burton. They were from the same hometown. The girl painted on the nose of the plane was a girl they both knew, Rose Price. They had named their plane *Tupelo Rose* in her honor, each hoping she'd choose him once they got home. By consent they'd taped her picture to the plane's control panel, for luck. Now

Tupelo Rose, her rudders useless, was grinding lower and lower, the pretty brunette on her nose destined for a fiery break up.

Burton emerged from the cockpit. He held up the photo of Rose, yellowed cellophane tape still stuck around the edges. "Who's taking her, you or me?"

Rose smiled out at them, straight white teeth and a cashmere sweater Danny had got his hand under once. The plane lurched. He grinned at Burton, hit him in the arm to say all he couldn't say. "You take the picture. I'm gonna get the girl."

Burton tucked the photo inside his jacket and jumped. Danny was right behind him. A trick of the wind carried Burton away, toward the river's far bank, until Danny could no longer make out the grainy silk of his chute. With Burton went Danny's luck, all of it, tucked into the four corners of that snapshot. Burton escaped that night. Flemish resistance smuggled him out. After he got back and finished his twenty-five bombing runs in a new plane, the Army Air Force sent him on a hero's tour that finished up in Tupelo, where he married Rose Price. *Life Magazine* published their picture. Danny spent the war in a POW camp. By the time he got home, Rose was pregnant with Burton's second child and the *S* shapes were jumping out at Danny everywhere, their repetition making him dizzy and sick.

"Danny? You all right?" Chase said.

Danny's hands trembled. He squeezed them together. "I'm good."

Burton was coming here to promote a Hollywood movie somebody had made about his escape. Coming with his wife. Not Rose Price, who'd died of an aneurysm years ago. Some other gal, a lot younger. And when they left, Danny was going with them, leaving the Victory Home for the first time since he'd arrived.

When Burton had first called, Danny couldn't imagine leaving. Burton's voice on the phone sounded the same as it had in the old days. "I want to talk to you about something, Danny. We make a nice living, my wife and I, making appearances at air shows. We even got invited to join a USO tour of Vietnam, though they're nuts to think I'd want to visit that hellhole. With this movie coming out, the opportunities are only going to get better. I want you to come with us. You and me. The pilot and tail gunner of the *Tupelo Rose*."

Danny appreciated the offer. Burton hadn't abandoned him all these years. He always sent a basket at Christmas when he knew where Danny was, and once wired the money to get Danny out of jail. But Danny couldn't leave the Victory Home. "I live here," he explained.

Burton didn't take no for an answer. He talked to Matron, and then to the Board, and the Board decided Danny should try it, just for the few weeks of the publicity tour. Matron gave Danny the news. He could tell from the look on her plain face that she didn't like the idea any more than he did.

"I just don't know that I'm ready," he said.

"Well, the Board thinks you are." She touched his arm. "It's going to be fine."

And by now Danny thought it would be fine. He felt strong. He'd practiced in his head how it would be, him and Burton together again like they had been early in the war. It was a chance to earn some money besides his disability check. A chance to get back some self-respect. He knew Burton had offered it because he felt guilty about being the one who escaped and got to have a life afterward, but Danny didn't begrudge him. He just wondered sometimes, about his luck, how it had all gushed away. But now maybe some of it was coming back.

Chase swung his legs to make the swing move. "I wish you weren't going away."

"It's not permanent. I'll be back before you know it."

"You sure are dressed up," Chase said. "I hate dressing up."

"I don't much care for it either." Matron had helped Danny with his clothes. Found a brown suit and shoes to replace the stained dressing gown and slippers he usually wore. Did the buttons for him and tied his tie. The shoes pinched and squeaked when Danny pushed off with his foot to get the swing going for Chase. The suit was hot. A drop of sweat dribbled from his forehead into his eye.

The town's police cruiser rounded the bend in the road, followed by a white Cadillac that looked brand-new, with a little American flag flying from its mirror. Burton. The cars parked at the curb. The police chief and mayor jumped out of the patrol car. The mayor hurried back to the Cadillac to open the passenger door. A woman got out, adjusting big aviator-shaped sunglasses on her nose. She was trim, with bright red hair swept off her forehead like Elizabeth Montgomery's on that *Bewitched* show. Her orange pantsuit had big purple flowers on it. Danny couldn't get used to pantsuits on women. She turned toward him. Her sunglasses tinted even darker in the sun, so Danny couldn't see her eyes. That bothered him, that she would want to hide her eyes.

Burton climbed out of the driver's side and stretched. He was heavier than last time, his sideburns longer. He saw Danny on the porch and waved, then saluted, a big grin on his face. Danny saluted back.

Burton and the woman walked up the steps to the porch. Burton's shoes came down hard on the wide boards, sending gray paint chips flying. Danny started to stand up.

"Stay put." Burton shook Danny's hand, slapped his shoulder. "It's been a long time, Danny Boy."

"Good to see you, Cap'n." Something swelled in Danny's chest, a feeling from the before times. He closed his eyes to enjoy it before it flew.

"He's a colonel now, not a captain," the woman said.

Danny opened his eyes.

"Danny, this is my wife, Annette," Burton said.

"It's a pleasure to meet you, Danny." She offered a hand, cool and lotioned, her grip not tight enough to keep Danny's own hand from shaking. There was something hard in her face.

Danny let go of her hand. "This is my friend Chase."

Burton shook Chase's hand. "How are you, young man?"

"Just fine," Chase said.

Annette called down to the police chief and mayor in the yard. "Can you nice gentlemen help me unload the car?" She left the porch to supervise, hips swaying left then right, pants stretched over her tight round rear. Burton gazed after her, a little smile twisting the corner of his mouth. "Isn't she a peach?"

Danny murmured something agreeable, remembering Rose Price. Rose never wore pants.

The police chief and mayor carried a folding card table and boxes up onto the porch. "People will start showing up here in a little bit," the mayor told Burton.

Annette began setting up the card table, snapping its metal braces into place and standing it upright before the police chief and mayor could offer to assist. She unpacked the boxes. Red, white, and blue bunting to hang on the front of the table. A microphone, the kind that didn't need a cord, like the one on TV where the guy in the convertible says, "Hey, good lookin', I'll be back to pick you up later." A big framed picture of Burton shaking hands with President Nixon in the oval office. Then a stack of photographs, all the same, of the crew of the *Tupelo Rose*. Danny was in the photograph, second from the left. He hardly recognized himself.

Matron came out to the porch. Danny stammered introductions. Matron raised her eyebrows at Annette's display. "My goodness. What have you got there?"

Annette opened a large photo album on the table, plastic sleeves holding pictures of merchandise. "It's our catalog. Lithographs. Limited-edition prints. T-shirts with the plane on them. I brought these for the kids." She hefted a cardboard box onto the table and opened it. Key chains, with *Tupelo Rose's* pin-up girl silhouette in red and pink plastic. "And we have these." She unrolled one of several paper tubes. "The poster from the new movie. Autographed by the colonel."

Matron smiled at Burton. "How exciting to have a movie made about you."

"Who's in it, Colonel?" the police chief asked.

"Ryan O'Neal as yours truly," Burton said.

"Who plays Danny?" Chase asked.

Burton's eyes flitted to Danny, apologetic. "Most of the story line is after I land."

Annette tapped the microphone and blew into it once to test the sound. "They show the crew parachuting out. The credits just say, 'Tail gunner, so-and-so.'"

Burton nodded at Danny. "Never was a better tail gunner. Danny got a Distinguished Flying Cross for taking out three Focke-Wulfs on one bombing run. Where's your medal, Danny? You ought to have it on today."

The Distinguished Flying Cross. Danny had sold it at a pawnshop outside Atlanta, his hands shaking so hard the owner took pity on him and gave him a couple more bucks than agreed. *Easy there, buddy.* Danny took the money next door to a liquor store and bought enough booze to black himself out for two days. He woke up on the sidewalk in front of an empty elementary school. An American flag whipped *S* shapes in the air, its cord slapping a rhythm against the metal flagpole.

"I must have misplaced it," Danny said.

People began to arrive, some driving up in their cars, others walking from town. They spread picnic blankets on the Victory Home lawn. Chase jumped off the porch to go play with other kids. The police chief and mayor left to help direct parking.

"I'm going to freshen up before everybody gets here." Annette went inside, leaving Burton and Danny on the porch.

Burton eyed the gathering crowd. "We're going to make a good team, Danny. Two autographs are worth more than one." He leaned closer, waving a thumb at the merchandise on the card table. "It's cash, mostly. No need to get the tax man involved."

Children squealed, chasing each other across the lawn. Chase's mother yelled for him to get down from a tree. Annette returned from inside, smelling of newly sprayed perfume, Lily of the Valley, the same scent Rose Price used to wear.

"I was just telling Danny how happy we are that he's joining us," Burton said. Annette didn't say anything.

The mayor and police chief came back and dragged white rocking chairs from the other side of the porch to seat Burton, Annette, and themselves in a row. Matron sat down on the swing next to Danny. "You okay, Danny?"

"Yes, ma'am."

"I've packed you some tuna sandwiches for the road. I'm proud of you. You're going to do great."

The mayor took the microphone and got people's attention. "We are honored today to have a true American hero as our guest. Colonel Mackie Burton is one of the most decorated B-17 bomber pilots to come out of the war. He's also the subject of a new feature film that'll be out in a few weeks, telling about him being shot down and escaping from the Nazis. I know all of y'all can't wait to see that. Colonel Burton is here today with his lovely wife, Annette. They chose to come here because our own Danny Marlow was the tail gunner on Colonel Burton's crew. Many of you know Danny. He's leaving us for a while, and I know you'll all wish him well." The mayor stopped long enough for people to clap. "So, without further ado let me turn the microphone over to the colonel."

Burton stood up and took the mike. He had a gut now that he hadn't had when they were flying, but the way he stood was so familiar, a cocky tilt of the hips that nobody had beat out of him. Even from the back Danny would have recognized him anywhere.

"It's an honor to be here today, with my friend and crew mate Danny Marlow. Let me say a few words about the plane and her crew, then I'll take your questions." Burton started in on a little speech that Danny guessed he had given before, about the plane and his wartime romance with Rose Price. Annette certainly seemed to have heard it before. Her little feet, in high-heeled beige sandals, tapped impatiently. The people on the lawn swatted gnats and sweated. Danny suddenly felt exhausted. He wished everybody would just go away.

Burton began to talk about the crew. Danny listened to him say their names. Three besides Burton got out. Six, including Danny, were captured and sent to the camps. Two they never found; they may have gone down in the river. And, of course, Sweeney. The iron hook at the end of the chain holding up the porch swing spelled an *S* at Danny. He reached out a palsied hand and covered it up, squeezing the cold metal.

Burton finished talking. "I'll be happy to take your questions now."

A man in the audience raised his hand. "Did they ever find your plane, Colonel?"

"If they did I never heard about it. It's a shame we lost her. She was a beauty." Burton pointed to someone else with a hand up.

Annette had sat still long enough. She stood up and got the stack of photographs and a permanent marker from the card table, then pulled her rocking chair over close to Danny. She set the stack of photos on the swing between Danny and Matron and sat down, talking in a low voice. "When he gets through answering questions, people are going to want these. Mackie has already autographed them. I want you to do the same." She took the cap off the marker, handed it to him, and put the top photograph on the arm of the swing for him to bear on.

Danny took the marker, but his hand wobbled. He was afraid if he touched the marker to the photo's glossy surface, he'd scribble all over it.

"Here. Let me." Annette grabbed his hand, her polished orange nails pressing into his skin. She directed him, signing for him. Reached for another photo and made him sign it, then another. The photograph showed the twelve crew members of the *Tupelo Rose* and their chief mechanic, standing in front of their plane at the base in England. They were all so young, just boys. Sweeney stood two men down from Danny, squinting at the camera, a big grin on his face. Annette gripped Danny's hand tighter. The marker's felt tip slid over the picture, drawing the loops of his signature. A thick black ink line swept right through Sweeney's face. Danny tried to pull away but Annette squeezed his hand harder. "P-please," he said.

"That's enough," Matron said.

Annette sighed. "Fine." She let go of his hand and went back to the card table. While Burton continued to take questions, she wrote out price tags. Dollar signs with two bars. She spread key chains out on the table to tempt the children. *Tupelo Rose* tucked her plastic knees under her, her body curving into an *S*. Danny's legs and arms started to shake. Matron moved closer. The stack of slick photographs cascaded off the swing onto the porch.

Annette looked up and saw Danny shaking. She grabbed the framed photo of Burton and President Nixon and hurried over to crouch in front of Danny with it, to hide him from the crowd. She whispered to Matron, "Can you take him inside? We can't have him acting like this."

Burton noticed something was wrong. He broke off talking and headed over to the swing. Annette stopped him. "I knew this wasn't going to work. You've done all you can for him."

By now Danny's shoulders were jerking. He couldn't breathe. He hugged himself, head down, trying to hold his body still. He could see Matron's shoes and stockings, the slight swelling at her ankles. She put her arm around his shoulders, using her weight to stop the swing from shaking. Chase bounded up the porch steps, the rubber soles of his tennis shoes slapping, and put a hand on Danny's arm.

Danny could sense Burton standing worried above him. He wanted to make Burton feel better, to tell him it wasn't his fault, but he couldn't speak. A teenaged boy in the crowd ignored the commotion with Danny on the porch and called out another question. "How'd you know which way to go when you landed, Colonel?"

Burton, reluctant, left Danny and returned to the center of the porch. He spoke into the microphone. "Son, I followed the river. That river saved me."

Wind lifted, moving sibilant through Ligustrum leaves. Danny raised shaking fingers and pressed them to his ears.

"I'm going to take you upstairs now," Matron said softly. "We'll unpack your suitcase."

"Danny," Chase said. "Remember something different." He took Danny's hand, squeezing it hard, and Danny squeezed back. He remembered a night in the prison camp when his group took revenge on a German shepherd that had terrorized them since their arrival. They salvaged a rare piece of meat from the day's stew. Danny went outside in the yard and waved it at the dog. When it chased him he ran into the barracks, where the rest of them were waiting. They let him in, then slammed the door on the dog's neck, almost decapitating the bastard.

"Little boy, you need to go back to your place," Annette said to Chase, still trying to hide them all with the photo of President Nixon.

Danny raised his head. "He stays," he said.

Burton set his microphone down on the card table. Annette fluttered her hands at him. "Keep answering questions!" But Burton offered Danny a hand to help him up, waiting until he was ready. Danny rested a palm on the top of Chase's head. He could feel warm oil at the roots of Chase's hair from all his running around. Danny's tremors began to subside. A last breeze whispered across the porch and he breathed it in before it disappeared. Above them an airplane droned, too far up in the white sky to see.

The Stole

The mink stole, with its red satin lining, lay in its box on the bed like a piece of expensive roadkill. The mothball fumes that rose from it were strong enough to burn Lorna's eyes. She reached out a finger to touch it, feeling lumpy seams under the fur. The lining had faded in places, the fancy name worn off the fraying label, but the fur itself was exquisite, so soft it almost wasn't there.

Her parents gazed down at it.

"I will not, under any circumstances, wear that thing," Lorna's mom said.

Lorna's dad blinked behind his glasses, the worry line between his eyes deeper than usual. "It's complicated."

Her mom shook her head. Dark brown hair fell over her shoulders. "That horrible old woman. She's only giving it to me because she knows her sister wants it. It smells. And those poor little animals."

"She especially wanted you to wear it to the fall gala," Lorna's dad said.

"She" was Mrs. Dolores Vaughan Parke, an old lady who gave a lot of money to the McMullen School. Mrs. Dolores Vaughan Parke and her sister, Mrs. Sheila Vaughan Emory, were co-presidents of the Atlanta Women's Club. Mrs. Parke was so bent over she was hardly taller than Lorna. A fascinating array of large moles showed through the white hair on her scalp. Mrs. Parke and Mrs. Emory couldn't stand each other and used the McMullen School as their tug-of-war rope.

Lorna's dad lifted the stole out of its box and draped it over his wife's shoulders. "At least try it on."

"It's molded itself to Mrs. Parke's shape," her mom said. "Look how rounded it is. It's trying to bend me over." Sure enough, when she stood up straight the stole puckered at both shoulders.

"If you don't wear it to the gala, you'll make her angry," Lorna's dad said.

"If I do wear it, I'll make her sister angry. Which one are you more afraid of?"

Lorna's dad sighed. "Maybe it will be unseasonably warm that night and you can use that as your excuse to leave it at home."

Lorna's mom took the stole off and dropped it back in its box. "I wouldn't be seen in that thing if it got cold enough to freeze hell."

Lorna sat down on her parents' bed and examined the stole's box, peering through the clear plastic window in the lid. "I could wear it," she said.

"Go get ready for school, Lorna," her dad said.

That Thursday morning Lorna waited for Chase outside their combined third and fourth grade classroom. He chugged up the hill, his mother yelling after him about his hair not being combed. He reached Lorna and they went inside together. The other five kids in their class were already sitting down.

Normally their teacher, Mrs. Dees, sat at her desk taking attendance, but today she had pulled out an audiovisual cart and had the TV on. Lorna's parents didn't allow her to watch unless it was something special like an Apollo mission. She scooted her desk closer to get a good view. A newsman was talking. Behind him, firemen hosed down a burning building.

"That's Cordelia," Mrs. Dees said. "Just twenty miles south of here."

"How'd the fire start, Miz Dees?" Chase wanted to be a fireman when he grew up.

"Some bad people firebombed the movie theater."

"Why come?" Mikey Domiano asked.

Mrs. Dees pressed her red, lipsticked lips together. "Some Black people were mad that the theater wouldn't let them in to see the movie."

"Oh, man. My mom was supposed to take us to see *True Grit* this weekend," Mikey Domiano said.

Lorna hadn't known there were enough Black people in Cordelia to do as much damage as showed on the news. There sure weren't many Black people in Tonola Falls where the McMullen School was. Mrs. Pickens, who ran the school cafeteria, and her family were the only ones Lorna knew. Mr. Pickens was a prison guard at the federal prison near Clayton. The Pickenses' seventh-grade daughter, Edwina, rode the school bus from her school in Clarksville to the McMullen campus every afternoon and did her homework in the cafeteria while Mrs. Pickens planned lunch for the next day. If Edwina got done early, her mother let her play with Lorna and Chase. Edwina was strong. She could swing them around by their wrists so they went airborne, though lately she said they were getting too heavy. The Pickenses' other daughter, Arabella, wasn't old enough for school yet.

The newsman on TV kept talking. "The theater's custodian suffered third-degree burns and has been taken to the burn center in Atlanta."

"Did they catch the people who made the fire?" Chase asked.

"Not yet," said Mrs. Dees.

"Why didn't the theater let the Black people in to see the show?" Lorna asked.

"It's hard to explain," Mrs. Dees said.

At supper that night Lorna's parents discussed the firebombing.

"What was that theater manager thinking. Did he never hear of the Civil Rights Act? Does he think back-country Georgia is somehow exempt from the laws of the United States?" Lorna's mom was from Pennsylvania and didn't think much of the south. If she ever heard Lorna slide into a southern accent or say "y'all," she corrected her.

"It takes time for people to change. Sometimes you have to have a few funerals first."

"That's ridiculous, Richard," Lorna's mom said.

"It doesn't affect us here, anyway, thank God," Lorna's dad muttered, cutting his pork chop.

"Well, there's a meeting about race relations tomorrow afternoon at the Unitarian church in Clarksville, and I'm going. Lorna, you can go home with Chase after school."

"Sarah, don't go getting involved in this," Lorna's dad said.

"Try and stop me."

"Dad," Lorna said, "why doesn't Edwina Pickens go to our school?"

Her dad looked over his glasses at her. "The lower school is for children of faculty only, honey."

"But the Domiano boys go, and their mother's a cafeteria lady like Mrs. Pickens."

Her dad chewed the inside of his cheek.

"Edwina's a lot smarter than any of those Domianos," Lorna said.

"An excellent point, Lorna," her mom said. "Just for that, you get dessert tonight." She got up and went into the kitchen in search of something sweet for Lorna's reward.

Lorna's dad cleared his throat and started to say something.

"Let me guess," said Lorna. "It's complicated."

"Don't get smart with me, young lady."

In the kitchen, Lorna's mom laughed.

Lorna couldn't wait to go home with Chase the next afternoon. Most days after school she'd be playing with Chase and the Domiano boys, and on the dot of three o'clock, no matter how good a game they were in the middle of, the boys would all run home to watch *Gilligan's Island*. Now, finally, Lorna could see the show for herself. She and Chase played with his GI Joes until three, then plopped down on their stomachs in front of the television. The castaways on *Gilligan's Island* were putting on a Shakespeare play, *Hamlet*. Just as Mrs. Howell was saying, "A ship! I see a ship in the harbor!" the television started to beep and the words "SPECIAL REPORT" came on the screen.

Lorna looked over at Chase. "What's it doing?"

"Aww, dooky," said Chase.

"Chase Robbins, I'll wash your mouth out with soap," his mother called from the kitchen.

"This is a News Four special report," said the announcer. "Police today have arrested five Black men and a white woman in connection with the firebombing of the Hampton Theater in Cordelia early yesterday morning."

Chase's mother came into the room, wiping her hands on a dish towel. "Thank goodness. Now we can all rest easier."

"One of the men taken into custody is the Reverend Alvie Davis, head of the Georgia Task Force for Racial Justice. All male suspects are being held at the Habersham County jail. The female suspect has been released on her own recognizance due to medical reasons, pending a bond hearing Tuesday. Now back to our regular programming."

Gilligan's Island came on again.

"We missed the best part," Chase said.

"I wonder what a white woman was doing mixed up in all this," Chase's mom said.

On Saturday morning, while all the other kids in the neighborhood watched cartoons and ate Lucky Charms for breakfast, Lorna stood on the broad flagstone steps of the administration building, playing Old Timey School with five-year-old Arabella Pickens. Arabella's mother had talked her husband into helping her lift heavy food boxes in the cafeteria. Lorna kept Arabella entertained while they worked. Arabella wore a blue sailor dress and shiny black Mary Janes, and her hair was plaited in three perfect, puffy braids, each fastened at the end with a blue plastic butterfly barrette. Lorna would rather have played with Arabella's older sister, but Edwina had a piano lesson.

To play Old Timey School, Lorna hid a piece of gravel in one fist, then held both her fists out to Arabella. If Arabella guessed which hand the rock was in, she moved up a grade by scooting up to the next step. Arabella was not very good at the game. She'd been stuck in kindergarten on the bottom step for the past five tries and was starting to whine. Lorna was bored. She knew Chase wouldn't leave his house to play until all the good shows were over at noon.

The cafeteria was right next to the administration building. Mr. Pickens came out the screen door that led to the kitchen and dumped a stack of empty cardboard boxes in the trash can. He walked up the slanted sidewalk to the front of the building where Lorna and Arabella were playing. Mr. Pickens was the biggest man Lorna had ever seen, with legs like the pillars on the front of the administration building. The prisoners he guarded at the federal prison were sure to listen when he told them to do something. His skin was lighter than Mrs. Pickens's skin and he had freckles across his nose. Lorna had never seen him smile. "We got to go in a minute, Arabella," he said.

"Wait for me to get to the third grade," she said.

Lorna put her hands behind her back, switched the piece of gravel from her right fist to her left, and held both hands out for Arabella to choose. She even held the rock hand closer to Arabella, to give the little girl a clue, but Arabella still slapped the wrong hand. Lorna opened her hands to show Arabella she'd chosen wrong.

Arabella pouted. "I'm never going to get out of kindergarten."

A car engine strained as it climbed the steep road to the school. Mrs. Dolores Vaughan Parke's big black Lincoln Continental drove slowly around the circle and stopped. Her driver, a Black man named William, got out and opened the rear door. Mrs. Parke climbed out, holding the door frame for support. The hem of her peach-colored suit skirt inched up, showing a stocking rolled down to the knee. She saw Mr. Pickens and Arabella standing on the stairs with Lorna and narrowed her eyes.

Mr. Pickens nodded to her. "Good morning, Miz Parke."

Her face relaxed. "You're Murial's husband."

"Yes, ma'am. She's inside doing inventory."

Mrs. Parke started for the stairs. Her right leg was shorter than her left, and she rolled with every step.

"You want me to walk you up, Miz Parke?" William said.

"I believe I can handle a few stairs. I'm not infirm." She reached the broad stone steps and grasped the metal handrail. Arabella moved to make room for her. Mrs. Parke reached out and patted Arabella on the head. "Aren't you a pretty little Ginger." Arabella, shy, hid behind Mr. Pickens.

"Is your father inside, Lorna?" Mrs. Parke said.

"Yes, ma'am."

Mrs. Parke made her way up the short flight of steps while they all stood holding their breath, afraid she might fall. She reached the top and crossed the stone patio, opened the heavy glass door of the administration building, and went inside.

William leaned back against the Lincoln, pulled a pack of Juicy Fruit gum out of his pocket, and offered it to Lorna and Mr. Pickens. Lorna took a piece even though it had sugar in it, figuring her dad would be tied up with Mrs. Parke for a while and would never find out.

Mr. Pickens unwrapped his piece and put it in his mouth, grumbling as he chewed. "Old white lady calling her Ginger, like every little colored girl's name is Ginger. Her name ain't no *Ginger.*"

Arabella swung out from behind her daddy's leg so William could see her. "My name's *Arabella.*"

"Now that's a pretty name for a pretty girl." William held the pack of gum out to her and she took a piece.

Mr. Pickens nudged Arabella. "What do you say to the man?"

"Thank you, sir." Arabella ducked back behind her daddy.

"I don't envy you having to drive that woman around. She act like her shit don't stink," Mr. Pickens said.

"Oh, it stink all right, but don't be too hard on her. She's had her share of troubles, family troubles, like all the rest of us," William said.

"If you say so. We better get going. I got some business in Cordelia this morning," Mr. Pickens said.

"You be careful. They mighty nervous in Cordelia right now," William said.

"That's why I'm carrying Arabella with me. White people ain't scared of a Black man got his little girl with him. Keep me from getting shot." Mr. Pickens put his big hand on the top of Arabella's head. "Come on, girl." He and Arabella headed down the incline toward their car, Arabella skipping to keep up with her daddy.

William held the pack of gum out to Lorna. "Take a piece to my buddy Chase."

Lorna took the gum and wandered down the hill, trying to think of something to do.

"What did Mrs. Parke want this morning?" Lorna's mom asked at supper that night.

"She wants extra security for the school, in light of the recent unrest," said Lorna's dad. "I told her the criminals had been caught and I didn't think we had to worry."

"They aren't criminals. There's no evidence against any of them," Lorna's mom said.

"Sarah."

"They're calling them the Cordelia Six," Lorna's mom said.

On Tuesday, Lorna and Chase's scout troops met at the community center in Clarksville. It was Lorna's mom's turn to drive them, in the red and white VW bus she had talked Lorna's dad into buying the year before. A million tiny holes patterned the VW's white vinyl ceiling. Lorna had pushed more than one toothpick into those holes. The two long seats in the back were movable. You could make them face each other, which is what Lorna's mom had chosen to do, or take them out altogether.

Lorna's mom dropped them off at the community center. When they got out of scouts an hour later she was parked at the curb waiting for them. Lorna and Chase ran over to the VW and opened its double doors to get in, then stopped. The fattest woman Lorna had ever seen sat in the back of the van, taking up the entire rear-facing seat. She was enormous, so fat her cheeks almost squeezed her eyes shut. Her black hair was thinning on top, like a man's. A plastic tube ran from her nose to a long green oxygen tank on wheels that leaned against the seat. The tank burped every few seconds.

"Lorna and Chase, this is Melody Haskell. We're giving her a lift to an appointment before we head home," Lorna's mom said.

Melody Haskell smiled and moved her oxygen tank closer to her swollen legs to make more room for Lorna and Chase. They climbed in and sat side by side on the seat opposite her.

"I sure appreciate the ride." Even those few words seemed to make her breathless.

"No problem at all," Lorna's mom said.

Lorna and Chase didn't know what to say. They sat quiet while Lorna's mom drove. Lorna tried not to stare at the lady, but Chase gazed at her with his jaw slack.

"Where do y'all go to school?" Melody Haskell finally asked.

"The McMullen School," Lorna said.

"I used to visit that school when I was a little girl," Melody said. "My grandmother would take me."

Lorna had a hard time imagining Melody ever being little.

Chase pulled two plastic soldiers out of his pocket and started banging them against each other, making them fight.

"Those are cool," Melody said. "Have you seen those new Weeble toys? They're so neat. 'Weebles wobble but they don't fall down.' I wish I had some."

Chase squinted at her, and Lorna could read his mind. Melody was shaped like a Weeble, and she wobbled. Hard to tell about the falling down part.

"Almost there," Lorna's mom said from the driver's seat.

Melody adjusted the oxygen tube in her nose and gathered up her handbag. Lorna's mom turned a corner and pulled up in front of the Habersham County Courthouse. She got out to help Melody Haskell. Melody got up. Where she had sat, the metal frame of the van's back seat was actually bent. The metal had torn away from the seat cushion, and some kind of scratchy stuffing poked out of the ripped upholstery. Melody eased out, gripping the edge of the door and stepping down one big leg at a time. Lorna's mom had a hand out, as if she could catch Melody if she fell. Once Melody made the pavement, she took a minute to get her breath, then lifted the wheels of the oxygen tank up over the curb to the sidewalk. "Thank you again for the ride."

"You're welcome. Good luck in there," Lorna's mom said.

Melody lumbered toward the courthouse entrance, where a crowd of people stood around. Lorna's mom shut the van doors and went around to the driver's seat. As soon as she was inside, Lorna and Chase asked at the same time, "Who was that lady?"

"One of the Cordelia Six," Lorna's mom said.

At home, Lorna and her mom found her dad outside on the patio, raking leaves into piles. The metal tines of his rake scraped over the patio stones.

Her mom explained where they had been. "The pastor asked me if I could drive her, since nobody else had a car big enough. She had to get to her bail hearing."

Lorna's dad stopped raking. "You gave a ride to a criminal, with two children in the car?"

"Her only crime is she's involved with a Black man," Lorna's mom said. "She's not dangerous."

"You don't know that. Good Lord, Sarah, how do you think it will look to the school trustees if they find out you've been helping one of the Cordelia Six?"

"I don't believe she was involved. She was as nice as could be, wasn't she, Lorna?"

Lorna shrugged. "I don't think she's a fire bomber, but she did break the back seat."

"What? Oh, for Christ's sake," her dad said.

"It's no big deal. It'll bend back," her mom said.

The phone rang and her mom went inside to answer it. Lorna's dad started raking again, hard, scraping the rake over Lorna's shoes so she had to move. Her mom came outside.

"That was the pastor. The judge denied bail for the five men. He set Melody's bail at five hundred dollars because she's charged with accessory after the fact, but she doesn't have that much money."

Lorna's dad leaned on his rake. "That's too bad."

"Don't pretend you care, Richard."

Lorna imagined Melody Haskell spending the night in jail, her fat hanging over the sides of her cot. She hoped Melody had enough oxygen in her tank to last until she got out.

On Thursday after school Lorna and Chase jumped in the leaves her dad had raked, until Chase got bored and started asking if it was time for *Gilligan's Island* yet. Lorna thought fast to keep him from going home. "Let's play suffragette."

"Huh?"

She pulled leaves out of her hair. "Come with me." She led Chase inside to her parents' bedroom, where the bed was half made. She dragged a chair over to the closet and stood on it to get down the windowed box that held the mink stole. She set it on the bed and opened it, stepping back so Chase could get the full effect.

"What is it?" he said.

"A mink stole." She said it with reverence, so Chase would know he was supposed to be impressed.

He wrinkled his nose.

"The suffragettes, the women who fought for the right to vote, always wore these." Lorna's mom had once taken her to the school librarian's house to watch a drama about women's suffrage on public television. "I'll be the suffragette, and you be the jailer who's locked me up."

The jailer part got Chase interested. "I need some keys."

"Just pretend." Lorna lifted the stole out of its box and swung it over her shoulders. It was heavier than she expected, and dust specks floated up from it, tickling her throat. She raised her arm, pointed an accusing finger at Chase and said in her best British accent, *"You have been forcibly feeding Mrs. Pethick-Lawrence!"*

Chase looked around. "Where can I lock you up?"

They heard the front door open and Lorna's mom came into the bedroom. "Lorna, take that fur off. It isn't a plaything." She held out her hand.

Lorna shrugged the stole off and gave it to her. "You weren't using it."

"Oh, I'm going to use it. Chase, would you like to come with us to Franklin?"

"Sure," Chase said.

"We'll be back before your mother knows you're gone."

"Why are we going to Franklin?" Lorna said.

"Just an errand." Her mom folded the stole, put it back in its box, and carried it out to the van.

Lorna's dad had taken the broken seat out of the VW to fix it, leaving open floor space in the back. Lorna and Chase took turns surfing, standing up on the ribbed rubber floor mats and trying to keep their balance as Lorna's mom drove the winding highway through Rabun Gap to Franklin. They passed a lone Esso station. Plastic letters on a portable sign out front spelled, "Jesus saves. Buy Tires." The VW bus's loud engine sent sound knocking between the red clay banks that collapsed into ditches on both sides of the road.

When they got to downtown Franklin, Lorna's mom made a hard right into a parking lot, sending Lorna and Chase tumbling. They climbed up from the floor of the van. A sign above the door of a one-story aluminum building said, "Casey's Jewelry and Pawn." Bird nests spilled out of two of the letters. They followed Lorna's mom inside the building. It smelled of cigarette smoke. All kinds of things were stacked up around the place. Musical instruments, guns, television sets. Chase picked up a ukulele and plucked at the strings.

A man came out from the back of the shop. He was older than Lorna's mom. Little red veins, like sewing thread, spread from his nose to his cheeks. He gave Chase a mean look, and Chase put the ukulele back where he'd found it. "Can I help you, ma'am?" The man didn't sound like he felt like being helpful.

Lorna's mom gave him a slow smile. Her front teeth were small and perfectly straight. "Are you Mr. Casey?"

"Casey expired three years ago. I bought the place." He didn't offer his own name, but Lorna's mom didn't let it faze her.

"I'm interested in selling this." She opened the box to display the mink stole. "If I can get a good price." She stretched out the *i* in *price*, sounding just like she was from Georgia instead of Pennsylvania.

The man fingered the fur.

"That's top-quality mink," Lorna's mom said.

"The style is too old-fashioned."

"A lot of women like that vintage look," Lorna's mom drawled. "Or someone could remake it, I understand people do that."

"Best I could do is a hundred and twenty-five."

Lorna's mom moved closer to the counter. She lifted her hair off her neck and let it fall again, as if she were hot. The jasmine scent of the shampoo she used loosed itself around them. Some of the irritation left the man's face.

"I'm sure it's worth more than that," Lorna's mom said.

The man looked at her for a long moment, then sighed. "All right, two-fifty."

She reached over to brush a piece of lint off the fur. The side of her hand touched his hand. "Three hundred."

The man who was not Mr. Casey opened his cash register and counted out bills. Lorna watched to see how much he was going to pay. One hundred. Two hundred. Two fifty. Three hundred.

Lorna's mom took the cash, fanning herself with the bills. "Thank you." She dropped the money in her purse. "Come on, kids." They followed her out. She trailed her fingers behind her as she walked, gently touching the surfaces of things: guitars, a glass case filled with old class rings, a typewriter. Lorna could feel the store owner watching her mom as they left.

Outside, they squinted in the afternoon sun. "I never saw a hundred-dollar bill before," Chase said.

Lorna peered into her mom's handbag. "That's a lot of money. What are you going to use it for?"

Her mom smiled down at her. "I'm going to bail Melody Haskell out of jail."

Friday was the annual McMullen School fall gala. When Lorna got home from school her maroon velvet dress lay on her bed, but her mom wasn't home. She still wasn't home when Lorna's dad got home around 4:30.

"Where's your mother?"

"I don't know."

Her dad took a shower and dressed in his tuxedo. Lorna heard him in his room, swearing about her mom being late.

At five-fifteen they had no choice but to set off for the gala without her mom. In the school auditorium, Mrs. Dolores Vaughan Parke and her sister Mrs. Emory were giving loud instructions to the caterers from opposite ends of the room. Round tables had been set up for dinner, and ladies from the Atlanta Women's Club fussed over the centerpieces, arranging and rearranging fall-colored plastic leaves and Indian corn.

Mrs. Parke, in a blue velvet dress and pearls, made her way over to them. "Where is your lovely wife, Headmaster?"

"She's getting ready. She'll be here shortly."

"I can't wait to see her in my mink." Mrs. Parke cut a sneaky look over her shoulder at her sister. Lorna guessed that what Mrs. Parke couldn't wait to see was Mrs. Emory's face when Lorna's mom walked in wearing the mink, though that wasn't going to happen since the mink was at the pawn shop in Franklin.

Lorna's dad looked like he felt a little bit sick.

Guests began to show up, and Lorna stood with her dad near the front door to greet them. The rich Atlanta people wore tuxedos and floor-length gowns. Faculty members did the best they could but looked drab in comparison. Chase's family arrived. His father had on brown pants and a plaid sports jacket. His mother wore a long pink dress with a pointy bosom that

Lorna happened to know was the matron-of-honor dress from her sister's wedding. Chase wore a suit, looking miserable, his red hair plastered to his scalp with water. Only Chase's older sister, Mandy, looked comfortable, in last year's baby blue prom dress. She set off immediately to find other people, boys, her age.

"Thank you for coming," Lorna's dad said, shaking Chase's dad's hand.

"Oh, was it optional?" Chase's dad looked around. "Where's your better half?"

"On her way." Lorna's dad turned to greet the next guest.

Chase and his parents eased toward a table not far from the front door, where Mrs. Emory ladled punch from a crystal bowl into glass cups. Lorna wished she could go with them but didn't want to leave her dad all on his own. It began to get dark outside and the stream of guests thinned. Just as her dad was telling one of the caterers to close the front doors against the evening chill, Lorna's mom arrived.

She looked stunning, in a slinky silver dress with a tiny beaded purse to match. Her hair was up in a French twist, with tendrils curling loose along her neck. She looked back over her shoulder as she came through the door, beckoning someone to follow her. Melody Haskell, in a red and white flowered muumuu too light for the cool weather, entered the auditorium, pulling her oxygen tank behind her.

Lorna's dad stared. Lorna's mom brought Melody Haskell over to where Lorna and her dad stood. Before Lorna's dad could say anything, Lorna's mom said, "I had to bring her. She had nowhere to go once I bailed her out of jail."

"You bailed her out of jail?!"

"Hush." Lorna's mom smiled and waved to someone she knew across the room.

"Where did you get the money for her bail?"

"She had some money," Lorna's mom said vaguely. Melody stood behind her, looking wan from her days in jail, and uncomfortable, like she thought she should apologize for being there.

Around them, people started whispering as they recognized the white woman from the Cordelia Six. Guests moved back, away from Melody, leaving an open space in front of the table where Mrs. Emory poured punch.

Mrs. Emory looked up. Her face stayed the same except that her drawn-on eyebrows lifted up almost to her hairline. Melody stared back at Mrs. Emory. The crowd had stopped talking. Melody's oxygen tank burped in the silence.

Mrs. Emory set down the glass cup she had just filled with punch. "Why, Melody," she said, sweet as pie. She turned her head over her shoulder and called out to Mrs. Parke across the room, "Dolores, I believe there's somebody here to see you."

The crowd parted for Mrs. Parke. Her orthopedic dress shoes, with pilgrim buckles, clumped as she made her way across the auditorium's hardwood floor. She got as far as the punch table and saw Melody Haskell. Mrs. Parke blinked, her head wobbling a little on her neck.

Melody stood there with her arms hanging, looking clumsy and a little scared. "Hello, Grandmother," she said.

Lorna's dad looked at her mom. Her mom shrugged, as surprised as everyone else.

Mrs. Parke reached a spotty hand out to clutch the edge of the punch table. Lorna's dad rushed over to pull up a metal folding chair and she sat down, hard.

"Punch, Dolores?" Mrs. Emory said. Mrs. Parke took the cup her sister offered and brought it to her lips, then set it back down again. "I'm afraid I'm not feeling well. I'd like to go home now."

"Somebody go get her driver," Lorna's dad said. Chase's dad went outside to find William.

Mrs. Parke struggled to her feet and smoothed the skirt of her gown.

"Mrs. Parke, why don't you wait here and rest while William brings the car around," Lorna's dad said.

"I can walk." Mrs. Parke waved away the arm he offered.

"I'll walk with you," Melody Haskell said in her breathless

way. She moved close to her grandmother, right arm ready to grab Mrs. Parke if she fell, left arm pulling the oxygen tank. The two of them shuffled toward the front doors. Lorna and Chase ran over and pushed the heavy doors open, holding them so Melody and Mrs. Parke could pass through. Outside, autumn wind blew Melody's thin dress around her legs and threatened to push Mrs. Parke over. Dry leaves scuttled across pavement. Mrs. Parke took Melody's arm for support. William pulled the car around and its headlights created shadow women, one hulking, one stooped and frail, until the spaces between them disappeared and they became one creature.

Once and Always

The Clarksville, Georgia, VFW post looked like every other VFW where Mackie Burton had ever pulled up a stool. Low ceiling, dark paneling, smoky, framed photos of aging vets hanging not-quite-straight on the wall behind the beer taps. It was cleaned to a male standard, the bar slightly sticky when he rested his elbows on it. At three o'clock on a Thursday only three men graced the place besides Mackie and the quartermaster-bartender. No women, thank God. These days in the bigger cities men brought their wives and girlfriends, raising the decibel level and complicating things. Mackie preferred it just to be boys, men like him who had seen action and appreciated his stories, who knew who he was or were impressed when they learned. His wife, Annette, was at home in Atlanta, and Mackie had dragged out his trip to north Georgia an extra day to avoid her. He had completed twenty-five bombing runs over Europe and once parachuted out of a crippled plane behind enemy lines, but Colonel Mackie Burton, U.S.A.F., Retired, was afraid of his own wife.

Mackie had stopped by this VFW partly because he got lonely on the road, and partly to promote the movie that was soon to hit theaters, about the plane he flew during the war and her crew. The movie bore the same name as his plane, Tupelo Rose. Mackie had named the plane after the girl who became his first wife, and his crew had painted a flirty pinup of Rose on the B-17's nose. The better the movie did, the more memorabilia Mackie could sell at flight shows and other appearances, his main source of income these days. He'd brought in a signed photo of his crew to give to the quartermaster, as he did at every VFW he visited. The fellas appreciated it, and the photo usually guaranteed that Mackie's drinks would be on the house.

The quartermaster set another Scotch in front of Mackie without his asking. The quartermaster had done his time in Korea, as had the quiet, ponytailed biker at the far end of the bar. The two guys perched closest to Mackie had both served in World War II, one in Europe like Mackie, the other in the Pacific. Mackie rarely saw any young men at the VFWs. The soldiers coming home from Vietnam now seemed ashamed somehow, as if they didn't feel entitled.

"Looking forward to seeing your movie, Colonel," the guy next to Mackie said. "You think they got it right? Some of those Hollywood war pictures just make stuff up."

"It's pretty much on target," Mackie said, thinking that the movie at least made him look good. "Except the inside of the *Tupelo Rose* looks like a damn luxury liner, space you wouldn't believe, not like a real B-17."

"They crammed us in like sardines, didn't they?" The other WWII vet patted his belly. "Lucky I was skinnier then."

"Weren't we all," Mackie said.

An old Zenith television sat on the end of the bar. The picture rolled annoyingly and the quartermaster had turned the sound down, but now the biker turned it up, to a special news report about the Cordelia Six. The Six were the big story in Clarksville and surrounding towns, five Black men and a white woman accused of firebombing a theater in Cordelia after the manager refused to let in some Black teenagers. A custodian who'd been caught in the fire had just died after lingering in the burn center for a few weeks, so the men were now charged with murder as well as arson, and the woman for accessory. One of the men arrested was a preacher from Atlanta, Alvie Davis, who was supposed to believe in non-violence, but the other defendants didn't make that claim.

On screen, a lawyer for one of the men stood on the steps of the county jail in Clarksville. "My client, Reginald Aldritch, is not a murderer," he said. "He's a decorated war veteran. The army awarded him a Silver Star for valor for saving three other soldiers during a firefight in Phuoc Long Province, Vietnam."

"You know what that means, don't you?" the WWII vet farthest from Mackie said.

"What?" said Mackie.

"It means if they execute that boy, he can be buried in Arlington Cemetery just like you and me."

"Now that ain't right," the WWII vet said.

"Damn straight," the quartermaster said.

"I don't know about that," Mackie said. "The boy served his country. He earned that medal. Punish him, sure, but you can't take that away from him."

"Killing somebody cancels out any honor he might have stored up, if you ask me," the guy next to Mackie said. "I got buddies buried in Arlington, men who died for this country. I don't want that criminal lying beside them."

The biker, who'd been drinking silently most of the afternoon, spoke up. "I'm with the colonel on this one. You get a honorable discharge, you get a doggone Silver Star, you got a right to be buried in Arlington even if you do go straight there from the gas chamber. Nobody told me when I got out of the army that I had to behave for the rest of my life. If they had, I'd a told them to kiss my sweet ass." He burped.

The quartermaster, behind the bar, shook his head. "That don't sit right with me." He fumbled under the counter and pulled out several sheets of paper and a clipboard. "I'm starting a petition, right here and now, to keep that boy out of Arlington Cemetery."

"While you're at it, make him give his medal back," the WWII vet said. "I'll be the first to sign." The quartermaster handed him a pen and he signed his name, hard and fast, then offered the pen to Mackie.

"Can't do it, gentlemen," Mackie said. "That boy saved his pals during wartime. He did what he did. It's permanent."

He drained the rest of his Scotch and pulled out his wallet to pay, but the quartermaster waved his money away. "We're honored to have you here, Colonel."

At the Howard Johnson's where he was staying, Mackie called Annette on the room phone, half hoping she wouldn't answer. By this time of day she would already have had three or four vodka tonics, growing more shrill and dangerous with each one. Annette threw things when she was drunk. She'd gotten hold of his pistol once and actually shot herself in the thigh, a quarter-inch graze that they didn't report. She'd been aiming at Mackie's dog, Blue. A woman who would hurt your dog would just as soon kill you. After that Mackie had given his pistol, and the dog, to his brother for safekeeping.

She answered the phone, her "hello" slurred.

"It's me, honey."

"Oh. Thought you'd finally call, did you?"

"I tried last night, and you didn't answer."

She was silent.

"I'll leave here tomorrow afternoon and meet you at the movie premiere like we planned, then we can go home and relax, just the two of us," he said.

Something crashed at her end. "Goddamned phone cord," she said.

"Annette?"

She hung up.

Mackie took his shoes and socks off and lay back on the bed. The motel room smelled of old cigarette smoke and the bug spray he'd caught the manager squirting outside his door that morning. He thought of his first wife, Rose, the disappointed crease between her eyes when she realized the flyboy she'd married was just a man, and not a very admirable man at that. The mix of disgust and resignation on her soft face at his womanizing. Mackie hadn't had to admit to the failure of his first marriage because Rose died of an aneurism before she got around to leaving him. Now, for better or worse, he had Annette.

The next morning, Mackie went to see Danny Marlow. Danny was the main reason Mackie was in north Georgia at all. The tail gunner on the *Tupelo Rose*, Danny had once rivaled Mackie for Rose's affections. Mackie won the girl, and Danny's prize for playing was two years in a German POW camp. Maybe it would have been better for all of them if Danny had ended up with Rose. The war, and the booze Danny paddled around in afterward, had done a number on him. He lived permanently at a home for alcoholic men, sitting on the porch, just trying to hold himself together. Mackie tried to get up to check on him when he could.

On his way to the Victory Home, Mackie stopped to get gas and pick up a carton of cigarettes for Danny. At the cash register, the clerk pushed customers to sign a copy of the petition to bar Reginald Aldritch from Arlington Cemetery. She'd taped Aldritch's mug shot to her cash register to scare people. The boy did look mean. He wasn't smiling, but then Mackie wouldn't smile either if he'd just been arrested. When it was Mackie's turn to pay, the clerk asked him if he wanted to sign and he just shook his head. It bothered him how fast that petition had taken off. The clerk already had four pages of signatures, the older pages curling under the newest one.

On the Victory Home's wide, columned porch, Danny sat in his usual spot on the swing, wearing a bathrobe and bedroom slippers. He was barely fifty but looked like an old man. Indian summer was in full session and the late morning sun burned low, lighting up the reds and yellows of the trees on the mountains. This was pretty country, more pleasing to the eye than the Mississippi flats where Mackie and Danny had grown up, but soon winter would set in. Mackie wondered what Danny did when it was too cold to sit on the porch.

Danny greeted him, holding out a trembling hand. Mackie gave him the cigarettes and sat down in a rocking chair next to the swing.

"Some of the fellas here are planning on taking a trip to see your movie," Danny said.

"How about you?" Mackie said.

Danny shook his head. "Matron doesn't think it would be a good idea, you know, seeing the plane go down and all."

"That's all right. You were there for the real thing. You don't need to see a movie about it," Mackie said. It didn't take much to set Danny off, poor bastard. Any reminder of the war seemed to ignite firecrackers in Danny's head. Mackie didn't think about the war much, and he believed that was why he'd been able to come back and function. He looked ahead, the way he had out of the B-17 cockpit window all those years ago. It was the pilot's job to look forward. It was the tail gunner's job to look back.

"You heard anything about this Cordelia Six?" he asked Danny.

"Some fella came by yesterday evening with a thing for us to sign," Danny said vaguely.

"Did you sign?" Mackie asked.

"No. I can't speak to what another man deserves or don't deserve." Danny tried to work the carton of cigarettes open. "Besides, my hands are too shaky to sign much."

Mackie took the carton from Danny and removed a pack, tapping out a cigarette for his friend. "You reckon those six are guilty? There's signs all along the road. *Free the Cordelia Six. Fry the Cordelia Six.* Take your pick."

"I don't know," Danny said. "Sometimes the truth camps out somewhere in the middle." He fumbled a lighter out of his pocket and managed to light up. "'Course, sometimes the truth ain't there at all."

Mackie left the Victory Home and headed into downtown Clarksville to find some lunch. He had to slow down in a traffic tangle around the courthouse and jail, where a crowd of Blacks and hippies protested with signs. While he waited for the cars ahead of him to move, he looked up at the barred windows of the jail. Reginald Aldritch was in there somewhere, while the people outside shouted back and forth about whether to erase who he'd been before the firebombing. Mackie wondered who he himself would be if somebody erased the part of him that had flown the *Tupelo Rose*. Some days he had trouble believing he had ever been that young man from Mississippi who took the world by the tail. Annette was good for that, whatever her problems might be. She didn't let people forget what Mackie had done, with the personal appearances, the limited-edition prints, and now the movie. And she didn't let him forget, either, when they were alone and he was feeling low and just needed her to rub his shoulders or pretend he was twenty again.

Traffic started to roll. Mackie thought about parking his car and going in to visit Reginald Aldritch. To let him know not everybody agreed with the petition, that he, Colonel Mackie Burton, didn't cotton to taking away what a man had earned in wartime. He couldn't quite imagine how that conversation would go, so he drove farther on and found a bar that served food.

The bar was a good choice, the first place Mackie had been where people weren't all tied in knots about the Cordelia Six. Mackie told the bartender who he was, and soon a friendly audience gathered. He had a few drinks and got a little more buzzed than he'd intended. He was feeling good, pumped from all the attention, then some idiot asked where his movie was going to show in Cordelia, since the theater was still a burned-out shell, and that got everybody talking about the petition again.

Mackie excused himself to use the bathroom. There was a pay phone next to the men's room, and after he peed he dug change out of his pocket and fumbled the receiver off the hook. He reached the operator and asked her to connect him to Arlington National Cemetery.

A sleepy voice answered. "Interment Service Branch. Lieutenant Dalton speaking."

"This is Colonel Mackie Burton. I'm calling about the burial of Reginald Aldritch at Arlington Cemetery." Mackie leaned against the wall to keep from swaying.

"Colonel?" The lieutenant sounded wide awake now. "What unit are you with, sir?"

"I'm retired," Mackie said.

"Oh." The lieutenant seemed to relax. "Are you arranging burial for a loved one?"

"No. I'm calling about the brouhaha here in Georgia. They've got a petition going to deny Arlington burial to this colored boy, Reginald Aldritch, who's about to go on trial for murder. I just don't think it's right. Y'all need to head it off at the pass."

"Is this man deceased?" the lieutenant asked.

"No, not yet," Mackie said, irritated.

The lieutenant paused before he spoke. "Sir, this is the Interment Service Branch. We bury people. Dead people. May I suggest you contact your congressman?"

Mackie gripped the phone. "Do you know who I am, son?"

"I'm sorry I haven't had the pleasure, sir."

"They just made a damn movie about me," Mackie said. The lieutenant didn't answer. Mackie slammed down the phone. Army red tape, same as when he was in the service. He went back to the bar and paid for his lunch, since nobody volunteered to buy it for him.

Back outside, he got in his car and drove back the way he had come. The crowd in front of the courthouse and jail had thinned some. He really ought to just go see that boy, talk to him. He remembered Reginald Aldritch's mug shot from the gas station that morning, his dark skin made even darker from photocopying, fierce eyebrows slanting down. Aldritch looked like a criminal.

Mackie passed the courthouse and drove a few more blocks, stopping at the railroad tracks for a three-car Norfolk Southern to pass. Some hippie had spray-painted words on one of the rust-colored train cars, "What if they held a war and nobody came?"

Mackie waited for the crossing gate to rise. He had dropped God knows how many tons of bombs on Hitler's Germany, returning to base countless times with pieces of his plane nicked off. He had survived a crash on a landing field in England and pulled his navigator out of the wreckage, the man burned so badly the skin of his arm slid off in Mackie's hands like the peel of a boiled tomato. And Mackie didn't have the balls to go talk to a colored boy in some shit-hole county jail.

He turned the car around and drove back to Clarksville.

Pale green paint flaked from the upper corners of the jail elevator. Mackie rode up in silence with a big sheriff's deputy, watching beams go by through the fingerprint-smeared Plexiglas of the elevator's tiny barred window. The jail's bleachy smell didn't quite cover the tang of urine. Mackie's celebrity had gotten him in. Now he just needed to figure out what to say.

The deputy led him into a room with a long table and two plastic chairs. Reginald Aldritch sat at the table wearing short-sleeved prison stripes, his hands cuffed in front of him. Light from a high window gleamed off his brown face. Each tiny coil of the man's hair seemed set to spring. His bulging upper arm bore an ugly keloid brand, of a Greek letter Mackie had forgotten the name of. Another scar, this one wild, from a rip or tear, peeked from his collar. The scar showed on Aldritch's skin in a way it wouldn't have on a white person. Mackie wondered what the rest of it looked like.

Mackie took the chair across from Aldritch. The deputy stood by the door, a big thumb touching his holstered gun. Mackie introduced himself and tried to think of a good way to start.

Aldritch looked at him impassively. "What is it you want, Colonel? Why you here?" His voice was lighter than Mackie had expected.

Mackie clasped his fingers together. "There's a lot of talk out there, about petitioning the government to keep you out of Arlington Cemetery. I don't know if you've heard it all."

"I've heard it," Aldritch said.

"Well, I've come here to say I don't think that's right. You earned your spot, and I'll do what I can to make sure they let you get buried there if that's what you want."

Aldritch's mouth opened a half inch. "Let me get this straight. You in here to make my funeral arrangements?" He shook his head in disbelief. "Mister, instead of worrying about where they going to bury me once they electrocute me, why don't you do something about me getting killed in the first place? Make a donation to my legal defense fund or something!"

"I didn't mean—"

Aldritch pushed back his chair and called to the deputy, "I'm ready to go."

The deputy unlocked the door and led Aldritch out, leaving Mackie in the room. Mackie could hear Aldritch as he walked down the hall, telling anybody who would listen, "Mother fucker planning my funeral."

It was time for Mackie to go home. He drove the narrow highway to Atlanta, red clay banks rising up on either side, trees still holding on to green as he traveled farther south. At the theater where the premiere would show, Annette was already set up in the lobby with all their merchandise out and ready, including tubed movie posters for Mackie to sign. Annette looked great, in tight pants and a silky flowered blouse, heels that tilted her forward so her cute bottom showed to maximum advantage.

There were other people around, the theater owner and the first of the moviegoers, so Annette gave him a big smile and kiss, and hung on his arm as the public gathered. She made him look good and Mackie relaxed, eating up the crowd, dealing out his autograph, shaking hands and comparing stories with any vets that came forward. The evening was fine all around, and it wasn't until the credits rolled in the darkened theater that Mackie began to brace himself for what things would be like at home.

He and Annette got back to the house hours past the time she would normally start drinking, and he could tell she was agitated. Without unpacking anything, she went straight inside and poured her first drink. From the foyer as he wiped his shoes he could hear ice cubes tinkling in her glass. He joined her in the dining room, and she handed him a vodka tonic, which he accepted. If you couldn't beat 'em, join 'em. Within a couple of hours she was sloshed, and her voice started to rise, berating him for things he had done or failed to do, for being gone too long, for being underfoot when he was home. On schedule, her anger turned to big, weepy tears, until she slapped a hand over her mouth and ran for the john.

Mackie followed her into the bathroom. Annette crouched over the toilet, heaving. Her first aim had missed. Vomit streaked the toilet rim and spattered the baseboards behind the john. "Oh, God," she groaned, spewing another round into the bowl.

Mackie reached over and flushed so she wouldn't have to smell her own stink, and held her hair back while she finished retching.

"You're a good man, Mackie Burton," she said, weeping again. "You deserve better than me." She wiped the back of her hand across her mouth.

He helped her up and supported her as she wobbled up the stairs to their bedroom. She fell onto the bed and lay still. Mackie spread a blanket over her and turned out the light, then unlocked the French doors that led to their balcony and went outside.

It was a night with a moon. Clouds billowed by in some celestial wind, though no breeze moved where Mackie stood. Mackie remembered it all clearly, even though he seldom turned his mind that way and the memories should have faded for lack of tending. The way his breath coned in the air at fifteen thousand feet. Each individual muscle in his hands, arms, and body that engaged to hold the yoke steady. The faces of every one of his men, those like him who survived when the plane went down, and those he never heard of again.

He stepped back inside, quietly closing the doors behind him. Annette slept, her mouth slightly open. He sat down on the edge of the bed. A strand of her hair was caught in the corner of her mouth. He pulled it away with his finger and stroked her hair, gently pulling out strips of drying vomit.

The Preferred Embodiment

The night his daughter Lorna was born, when Richard Pierce held her in his arms in the warmth of the hospital nursery, the promise he whispered to her was not *I will protect you* or *I will love you*, but this: *I will not embarrass you.*

His own father had made no such covenant. In the small Pennsylvania town where they lived in the years after World War II, his father was the man the neighbors stopped on the sidewalk to gawk at. His father, on the roof, clumsily bundling metal rods, plywood, sheets of aluminum, tilting mirrors to catch the sun. His father the inventor of things that didn't work. A solar oven that oozed underbaked cookie dough, antennae that didn't receive. Once, an automatic bird-feeding device that mangled a family of finches. His father threw the downy remains off the roof, arms raised and stained coat flapping as if he himself were some giant rumpled bird. Children gathered to watch, some perched on their bicycles, some leaping to catch the feathers that drifted through the air like dandelion seeds. Among them was pretty Becky Ames from next door, and Richard, mortified, hid behind a tree across the street from his house and didn't come out until porch lights winked on and parents called their children home for supper.

Richard's mother and his sister Mabe, large and laughing, thought his father was a card. They encouraged him, suggesting outrageous things he might invent for them. Super-girdles and love potion and permanent makeup that wouldn't wash off. Dust-resistant furniture. An electric doorbell to shock annoying salesmen. A contraption that would force the corners of Richard's sour mouth upward in a smile.

Richard left his father's house as soon as he could, earning a scholarship to prep school where rules offered peace, and no one invented anything. To stay in that ordered world he became a teacher and then the headmaster of the McMullen School. He made a perfunctory call to his father in Pennsylvania every Sunday afternoon when the rates were down, or had until recently when their conversations took a disturbing turn. For all his father's bizarre behavior, the man had always been happy. Now, stories Richard had heard his father tell the same way for decades began to feature new characters, new plot twists, all ugly and frightening. Happiness was peeling away from the nerve sheaths in his brain, flaking like the paint on Richard's boyhood home.

Mabe had moved the old man into a nursing home that month. "You should come up," she said the last time she called. "He wants to see you. There are things you might want from the house before we sell it."

"I'll try," Richard said, but he hadn't gone yet.

He stood, between tasks, at the kitchen window of the headmaster's residence. His daughter, Lorna, was out in the yard working on something with an intensity that would have made her grandfather proud. She measured a board the way Richard had taught her, his jigsaw lying beside her in the grass. Sunlight had found the auburn in her hair, and Richard felt the urge to put his hand on the top of her head in some kind of blessing or oath.

I will not stumble around on the roof. My feet will always touch the ground. I will not kill small animals in front of the neighbors. My clothing will be neither stained nor brightly colored. I will not forget to zip my fly. Where our house faces the street the paint will not blister and the grass will never grow above ankle height.

He went outside to where Lorna knelt, trying to cut the thick board with the jigsaw. Its flimsy blade bent, refusing to hold a straight line.

"What are you making?" Richard asked.

"A dunking booth. I'm going to have a carnival. Frankie Domiano has a rain barrel he's going to roll over here. I'm making the seat."

"Will you be the one getting dunked?"

"No, that's Frankie's job. I'm in charge of everything."

"I have a better saw for that. Want me to cut it for you?"

"Yes, please," she said. "I measured twice."

Richard got his saw and in just a few strokes cut through the wood along the penciled line she had drawn.

"Thanks, Daddy," she said.

"You might want to sand that end, so Frankie won't get a splinter."

She shrugged. "It's okay."

"When's the carnival?"

"Saturday after next. Will you come?"

"Does it cost anything?"

"A quarter for every activity. I'm saving for a model horse."

He resisted the urge to insist she give the money to UNICEF. "Wouldn't miss it," he said. The high school students at the McMullen School could afford to support his daughter's entrepreneurism. He helped her wedge the board into the crotch of a tree in the front yard, high enough off the ground that Frankie could jump off into the barrel. Then he stood back while she painted a red target on a piece of cardboard.

The last time Richard's father had seen Lorna she was a toddler. The old man had watched her playing with blocks on the floor. "We'll make an inventor of her yet!" he crowed. Richard froze, repulsed, and then filled with guilt. It was the same mix of feelings he experienced when he saw photographs of himself these days. When he smiled, showing his teeth, he looked like his father, and the revulsion that rose within him made him feel ashamed.

His jigsaw still lay in the grass where Lorna had left it. Richard picked it up. His father had taught him to use a saw like this. He remembered the feel of his father's callused hand over his, wrapped around the saw's smooth handle. The tickle of the blade's vibration in his palm. He went inside and phoned Mabe to arrange a date when he could drive up to Pennsylvania.

Every fall, the electric company invited the Tonola Falls community to a barbecue at the power station overlooking the gorge. The event was the McMullen School's best fundraiser, a chance for Richard to hobnob with company executives and rich alumni who came back each year for the pulled pork. At breakfast on the morning of the barbecue he looked at his wife and daughter with the eyes of a prospective donor, and found fault. Lorna hadn't brushed her hair, and the flowered bell-bottoms she'd pulled on, her favorite pair, were too short. Sarah was still in her bathrobe, no outfit selected yet, but Richard didn't want to leave anything to chance.

"Lorna, you'll need to change clothes before we go. That sweater Aunt Mabe sent you would be nice. And some longer jeans."

"That sweater itches," Lorna said.

"It's a barbecue, for God's sake," Sarah said. "No one will be dressed up."

"We need to look respectable. Casually respectable," Richard said. "The Vaughan sisters will be there, and some of our other biggest donors."

"Casually respectable." Sarah widened her eyes in mock horror. "Does that mean you might even go without a tie?"

"Please," Richard said wearily. People called Sarah a *free spirit*. They said it with fondness and even admiration, accepting behavior in her that they would never have condoned in a less attractive woman. Richard hadn't known about Sarah's free spirit when he got involved with her, hadn't seen past her lovely brown eyes and enticing curves. And perhaps she hadn't been so free then, but had only become so when she learned how uncomfortable it made him.

"Please," he said again.

"Relax," she said, turning away.

When it came time to go, Sarah and Lorna weren't ready. Richard didn't want to leave until he was sure they were presentable, but he couldn't be late.

"You go ahead. We'll be there shortly," Sarah said, brushing her long hair and shaking it into place.

He drove to the power station property. In the mowed field below the station the company had set up two pits with whole pigs and a separate wood fire for a cauldron of Brunswick stew, big enough for a child to stand in. The smell made Richard's stomach growl.

Several dozen people already sat on blankets listening to an impromptu bluegrass band. Richard shook hands with alumni he recognized, working his way across the field to where the power company president stood in front of a pile of hay bales with Mrs. Dolores Vaughan Parke and her sister, Mrs. Sheila Vaughan Emory. Both old women were swaddled in tweed. The sisters didn't like each other, and Richard had been known to make use of that fact, letting slip to one sister the amount of the other's pledge to get them bidding against one another.

Richard greeted the power company executive and the sisters and raised his hand to shield his eyes from the bright sunlight.

"I believe this is the nicest day we've ever had for the barbecue," Mrs. Emory said.

"Nonsense," Mrs. Parke said. "I distinctly remember at least two other Indian summer days nicer than this one. The colors just don't seem as vibrant this year." She swept an arthritic hand toward the ridge above the gorge, where trees burned with heartbreaking hues of red, orange, and yellow.

"Your eyesight's just dim," Mrs. Emory said.

As the sisters bickered, Sarah's VW bus drove into the gravel parking lot. Sarah and Lorna climbed out. Lorna, wearing her new sweater, immediately ran to join other children who had lined up to take a turn stirring the kettle of Brunswick stew with a canoe paddle.

Sarah walked across the grass toward Richard. She wore a midriff top that showed her navel and jeans with a hole in one knee so big it was a wonder the pants leg hadn't fallen off. The hole gaped like a talking mouth as she walked. A red bandana-print patch covered the other knee. The fronts of the thighs were worn so bare Richard could see flesh between the individual threads. Bleach spots dotted the pockets. Richard hadn't known she even owned a pair of jeans that ragged. He suspected she had borrowed them from a student just to sabotage him. He wished he hadn't said anything to her about what to wear. If he had just kept his mouth shut, Sarah's natural vanity would have led her to put on something nice. Their marriage had passed the point of even the simplest consideration for each other's feelings.

She reached them and gave the sisters and the company president a radiant smile.

Mrs. Parke arched a drawn-on eyebrow. "Richard, are we not paying you enough to clothe your family?"

"Oh, hush, Dolores. It's the style now," her sister said.

"I like the holes," Sarah said. "I'm getting a nice breeze."

"That's a mighty pretty knee," the power company president said, smiling.

"Why, thank you," Sarah said.

An employee brought over the first tray of fresh barbecue. Sarah wandered off to say hello to people she knew. Richard watched her walk over to where Art Robbins, the chemistry teacher, stood listening to the music. She put her hand on Art's arm, then looked over at Richard and deliberately moved closer to Art, facing him from just a few inches away. Richard could almost see Art start to salivate.

"Excuse me," Richard said to Mrs. Parke and Mrs. Emory. He walked around to the other side of the stack of hay bales and sat down on one, where no one could see him.

"In my day, men had control over their wives," he heard Mrs. Parke say.

"Oh, eat your barbecue, Dolores," her sister said.

Richard closed his eyes. He was having trouble drawing the heavy smells of pork and newly cut hay into his lungs, and his face and hands were tingling. His heart started to limp in his chest and he felt the falling sensation he sometimes experienced at night, that always made him think he was dying. Sweat dripped from his forehead into his tightly squinched eyes. Adrenalin gushed through his body, poisoning him.

"Daddy?"

Richard opened one eye.

"Are you sick?" Lorna said.

With effort, he reached out an arm and crooked it around her waist. "No, honey. I'm fine."

She put her arms around his neck and gave him a loud kiss that left a wet spot on his cheek. She smelled the same as she had since birth, of open air and a hint of maple syrup. The smell brought him back to himself and he was able to return her hug before she skipped off across the field to rejoin her friends.

I will not, Richard thought, but couldn't finish. *I will not. I will not.*

Richard made the long drive to Pennsylvania. Before going to the nursing home he went to his father's house, a one-story, identical to the others on the block except for the unmowed grass and the sag in the flat carport roof where his father used to test his inventions. Richard took the key from its place under the mat and went inside. He could tell Mabe had been in to clean, but clutter—things his father had gathered for projects he would never get to—lined the walls of the dim hallway. His father used Richard's old bedroom for storage and when Richard tried to push open the door, a dismantled metal bookcase fell with a clang. Tack holes in the wall, where Richard's Cleveland Indians pennant had once been, were the only sign that he had ever inhabited the room. He closed the door without going in.

In the small living room, behind his father's worn easy chair, family photographs crowded a built-in bookcase. Some were from his mother's era, nicely framed pictures of Richard and Mabe as children, but in front of them his father had lined up Lorna's wallet-sized school pictures in a colorful row. Sarah must have sent them in their Christmas cards. His father had laminated them in plastic to protect them, and Richard felt strangely touched.

On the middle shelf, exhibited like a diploma, was a familiar photograph of his smiling father holding the one patent he got on his only successful invention, a better chalkboard eraser. The patent itself was in a long, yellowed envelope tucked into the corner of the frame.

His father had been a manager at a janitorial company that cleaned office buildings at night. He noticed the janitors fighting over a certain type of sulfur-colored sponge, one they could use dry or wet, that devoured dust and dirty water alike. One night his father used one of the sponges to wipe the chalkboard in the break room where he listed assignments and was amazed when the sponge ate the chalk dust and didn't need dusting itself. He brought some of the sponges home and glued them to pieces of wood to make erasers, and emerged from his workroom announcing "the end of eraser-beating as we know it." Richard, who liked beating erasers for his teachers because it made him feel useful and special, was dismayed, but the things really worked. His father patented the eraser and had several thousand manufactured for sale. Richard's teachers loved the self-cleaning erasers and loved Richard's father. They got him to come in and talk to their classes about inventing. He demonstrated the eraser with a flourish and set off explosive science experiments while Richard sat stiffly at his desk.

His father, optimistic, resigned from his job to devote himself to selling the erasers, but demand wasn't what he had hoped. Money grew scarce. Richard's allowance stopped and his pants flapped two inches above his ankles because his parents couldn't afford to replace them. Finally, even Richard's jolly mother stopped laughing and his father went back to the janitorial company to grovel. The employer relented but made him work as a custodian for six months as punishment before returning him to management.

Richard eased the patent out of the picture frame. Moisture had resealed its envelope. He opened it carefully and extracted the patent. He could hear his father's excited voice in the old-fashioned language describing the patent's claims, its abstract, the field of invention, the prior art: "Commonly used chalkboard erasers, comprising laminated felt pads, are prone to the collection of chalk dust on the surface, causing the efficiency of the erasers to drop markedly in short order, and requiring frequent cleaning of the erasers." Under the heading, "Description of the Preferred Embodiments" he read, "The illustrative eraser consists of a resilient, porous, sponge-rubber body, affixed and generally coextensive with a handgrip member made of wood or other solid material. The body member shall have grooves extending lengthwise and disposed about its periphery."

Richard wondered if there were any boxes of erasers left in his father's basement that he might salvage for the McMullen School. He tucked the patent in his breast pocket, then opened the door to the narrow cellar stairs and pulled the chain to the overhead light bulb. Mabe hadn't cleaned down here. He waved an arm in front of his face to break spider webs as he descended the stairs.

Along the back wall, just as he remembered, were several unopened cardboard boxes of erasers. He stepped around and over piles of other items to get to them. The boxes had mildewed where they touched the wall, but he was hopeful that the erasers themselves would be intact. He ripped the seal off the first box and opened it. Surprised silverfish flowed outward like shiny drops of water from a fountain. Richard peered into the box. All that remained of the erasers was the wooden handgrip. The spongy body was completely gone, eaten by silverfish or dry rot.

All the boxes were the same. Richard left them where they were, not bothering to close them.

Back upstairs, he looked around the quiet house. His father's patent rustled in his breast pocket. There was nothing else here that he wanted. He started for the front door, then as an afterthought went back and retrieved the laminated pictures of Lorna. If his father didn't have space for them where he was now, Richard would take them home. Lorna grinned out at him from one of the photos, her two front teeth missing.

I will not fill our house with detritus that you will have to remove when I am old. I will do nothing to jeopardize my steady job. I will buy you clothes the other children will not laugh at. I will take care of our possessions, protecting them from rot and vermin.

At the nursing home, he found Mabe in his father's room, helping the old man eat supper. His father was wizened, no longer the big man Richard remembered from his last visit a few years before. When Richard took his father's hands they shook terribly, even when Richard squeezed them tight.

"Richie, I'm so glad to see you." His father's voice was a whisper.

"You too, Pop." Richard looked around. "I like your room."

"They take good care of me. Mabe takes good care of me. I get so tired that I can't do like I used to."

Richard brought out the laminated photographs of Lorna. "I found these at your house. Would you like to put them up here?"

His father looked puzzled.

"It's my daughter, Lorna," Richard said.

"Lorna," his father said. "Those were at my house."

"Yes."

"There's not much room here for personal effects," Mabe said apologetically.

"Then I'll just take them with me," Richard said, setting them on the bed.

"Pop, is that all you want to eat?" Mabe started to clean up his tray.

"I'd like some ice cream."

"I'll go get you some while you and Richard visit," she said.

"I don't want to be any trouble," his father said.

Mabe bent and kissed the top of the old man's head. "You're no trouble." She left to find an aide.

Richard's father lifted a trembling hand and wiped food from his chin. "There's something I have to tell you," he said.

"Sure, Pop," Richard said.

His father began a story Richard had heard him tell many times, of his childhood in North Dakota. Richard could recite it down to the last turn of phrase: a blizzard had left a drift of snow as high as their house against the front door. Richard's father, then four years old, hadn't understood and kept wheedling to go outside. Finally his mother, to tease, had said "go ahead." The boy had opened the door and faced a wall of snow.

Richard's father had always ended the story with the musical sound of his mother's laughter. But this telling was different. Someone else was in the snow-bound house now, a paternal grandfather, sinister in dark clothing, his face obscured by a wooly beard. The boy was alone with him, his mother and father stranded elsewhere by the snow, and the grandfather was doing awful things, unspeakable things, touching the boy in places he shouldn't, hurting him. Richard's father began to weep as he told it, his whole body shaking.

Richard stood rigid while tears and mucous streamed down his father's face. "He did bad things to me," his father sobbed. An odor of urine filled the small room. His father had wet himself.

Richard couldn't handle it. He left the room and leaned against the wall just outside his father's door.

Mabe returned, carrying a bowl of vanilla ice cream. She saw Richard's face. "Oh, dear. He's been telling stories. Which one? The snow?"

Richard nodded.

Mabe put a gentle hand on his arm. Her fingertips were cool from holding the ice cream. "It isn't true, you know. That grandfather died before he was born."

Richard couldn't speak.

"You get used to it if you're around him all the time," she said, with no hint of reproach. She took the ice cream into the room and Richard heard her murmuring to their father, calming him down. Richard took a deep breath and steeled himself to go back in.

I will not rewrite history, or if I do, I will paint it better than it was,

*not worse. I will not burden you with my baggage. The infection will stop
with me.*

He stayed in Pennsylvania just long enough to help Mabe
arrange the sale of their father's house, then drove home to
Tonola Falls, arriving in mid-afternoon. His yard was full of
people. Lorna's carnival. He had forgotten. He got out of the
car.

Frankie Domiano, the son of one of the cafeteria ladies,
was perched on Lorna's dunking booth, dressed like a clown.
A group of younger kids had created a freak show by drawing
masks in rough crayon on brown paper grocery bags. Sarah sold
paper cups of lemonade from a card table in the corner of the
yard. High school students had wandered over from the dorms
for the entertainment. In the midst of it all, Lorna directed the
show. Richard had never seen her look happier.

He walked over to her. "How's it going?"

"We've made twenty-four dollars and seventy-five cents so
far," she said.

A plump student tried her hand at the dunking booth.
Frankie taunted her, "Hey, fatso, can't get me! Fatty, fatty, two-
by-four!"

Richard called, "Frankie, that's not acceptable."

Frankie tried again. "Yah, yah, your pants are falling down!"
He cut his eyes over at Richard and Richard nodded.

"Are you coming to the carnival, Daddy?" Lorna said.

"Of course. Just let me wash up." He went inside and
splashed water on his face to get the road haze off, then went
back outside.

Lorna stood by the dunking booth, looking distressed.
Frankie Domiano was nowhere in sight.

"What's the matter, honey?" Richard said.

"Frankie quit. He went home to watch *Gilligan's Island*, so
now we don't have anybody to dunk."

"How about one of the other kids?"

"Their moms won't let them get wet."

"Then you can do it yourself."

"But I'm in *charge*," she said, her eyes welling up. "Could you do it, Daddy?"

"Me?"

"Please?"

Richard eyed the dunking booth. Lorna had filled the rain barrel with water from their garden hose. A few dead leaves floated on the surface. He looked at Lorna. Her lower lip trembled. She was fighting not to cry.

He sighed. "All right." He took off his shoes and used a low branch to pull himself carefully up to the seat in the tree, brushing flakes of bark off his clothes. The dunking booth worked on the honor system. If a beanbag hit the target, he was morally obligated to jump off the shelf into the barrel.

"Put the clown nose on." Lorna handed him the nose Frankie had worn, made with a long rubber band stapled to half a red rubber ball.

"Is that really necessary?" Richard said.

Her face said it was.

I will act my age. I will not behave foolishly. Richard stretched the rubber band around his head and centered the nose on his face.

"You have to yell things to make people want to dunk you," Lorna said.

Richard called out weakly, "Yah, yah." Nobody turned his way. Lorna began to look anxious.

Sarah flirted with a cluster of football players at the lemonade table. Richard cleared his throat and yelled to the quarterback. "Yah, yah, your pants are falling down!"

The quarterback turned around.

"You gonna take that, Bruce?" one of the other boys asked.

"Heck no." The quarterback swaggered over to the dunking booth. He dug a coin out of his pocket and handed it to Lorna. She gave him a beanbag. He slapped it from palm to palm, warming up, while his teammates cheered him on.

Sarah set the pitcher of lemonade down on the card table and crossed her arms to watch.

"You couldn't hit the side of a barn!" Richard yelled.

The quarterback wound up and hurled the beanbag expertly at the target, hitting the bullseye. His friends stood frozen, waiting to see what the headmaster would do. Lorna waited too, her body tense, her fist clenched around the quarterback's coin.

I will never look silly.

Richard took a breath and launched himself off the seat into the water.

Good Boys

Elena Domiano didn't know why it affected her so much, this boy dying. She had served him for three years on the cafeteria line at the McMullen School before he graduated and never had a real conversation with him. But he was a smiling boy, a kind boy, this Rob Whitaker, class of '69, and as Elena dished out vegetables to high school girls with bloodshot, mascara-smeared eyes, and boys with no appetite, she herself felt ripped open and raw. Killed in Vietnam less than a month after landing there. Elena, who was not a crier, couldn't look the students in the eye for fear of bawling. Instead she focused on a spot just beyond each one's left shoulder, breathing around the mass in her throat as she scooped broccoli casserole and creamed corn onto their plates.

A girl Elena had seen hang out with Rob Whitaker pushed an empty tray through the line. When Elena asked her choice of vegetable the girl shook her head and burst into tears. Her friends moved close, patting her shoulder, and led her away.

Elena remembered a day last year when she was serving with another cafeteria lady, Dot Hopkins. Dot was in her seventies. She came up to Elena's shoulder and was deaf as a rock. That day Dot's job was to serve rolls and brush liquid butter on them if a student wanted it. Dot had a sing-song going, asking each student, "You want butter on that? You want butter on that?" It drove Elena crazy.

Rob Whitaker came through with the rest of the football team, his hair still wet from a shower. "A roll, with butter, please," he said to Dot.

"You want butter on that?" Dot said.

The football player to Rob's left laughed out loud, but Rob just gave Dot a smile. "Yes, ma'am," he said, raising his voice so she could hear him.

Elena didn't recall ever seeing Rob be unkind. She wished she could say the same for her own boys. The two oldest were moving down the line now with the lower school classes. Frankie, twelve, was right behind nine-year-old Mikey, trying to step on the backs of Mikey's shoes to give him a flat tire.

The headmaster allowed Elena's boys to attend the McMullen School even though technically a cafeteria lady wasn't faculty. Thank God for it. She needed Frankie and Mikey to be where she could keep an eye on them. Frankie was a mess, always looking for a way to beat the system, and Mikey looked like an angel, with his curly blond hair and blue eyes, but he wasn't.

Frankie stopped fooling around when he got close to Elena.

"Don't think I didn't see you," she said, scooping corn onto his plate.

"What'd I do?" he said.

"Come right home after school," she said to both boys.

They pushed their trays past her down the line. In the back pocket of Frankie's Sears Toughskin jeans she could see the outline of a plastic army man he wasn't supposed to bring to school, the barrel of the soldier's green rifle sticking up above the pocket line. It reminded her of Rob Whitaker and made her sad all over again.

When she got off work that afternoon she walked home, across the playground in front of the cafeteria and around the circle of small faculty houses. It was only a little after three o'clock but already the sky had darkened, and the November wind chilled her through her coat. When her husband had left, stranding her with the boys in Tonola Falls, the headmaster had let her move into faculty housing. Without it she'd be screwed. The other faculty didn't include her in their social events, but she didn't care. She didn't have anything in common with those people anyway, being from the North, Italian, no college education. At least her boys were included, running in the gang of children. Not getting in too much trouble. Some, but not too much.

She reached their house, the last one on the circle, tucked into the woods past the headmaster's residence. The bike Frankie and Mikey shared lay on its side on the front steps, where anyone could step on it and break a neck. Elena moved it and went inside. Her sitter, Mrs. Hensley, an older lady from town, didn't mind staying with Elena's two youngest boys, Andy and Gordie, but nearly ran out the door every day after Elena paid her to avoid being there when Frankie and Mikey got home.

Mrs. Hensley held Gordie, the baby, nine months old. He was crying, that croupy cry of his. "He seems a little warm," Mrs. Hensley said, handing him off to Elena.

Elena touched her cheek to Gordie's. It did feel warm. "Please don't be sick again," she said.

"It's hard when the older ones bring the germs home," Mrs. Hensley said.

Gordon was the name Elena's husband had insisted on before he ducked out, a name too big for the little person it was attached to. Gordie was sickly, not growing like her others had. In a way she was relieved that he didn't crawl all over and climb, but she worried.

Andy, almost four, ran down the short hallway into the living room with an old towel clothes-pinned around his neck. "Thuperman!" he yelled. His diaper was so saturated it hung down nearly to his knees.

"He wouldn't let me change him," Mrs. Hensley said.

Andy was practically old enough to change himself. Before her husband left, Andy had been making good progress with the toilet training, not having many accidents during the day at all, but since Angelo had skipped out, Andy had regressed. He wasn't even trying anymore, though his brothers and the other kids made fun of him. And the pee and poop of a four-year-old was a lot more disgusting than Gordie's baby mess.

Mrs. Hensley left. Elena put Gordie in his playpen and went into the bathroom, yelling for Andy. "Andy, we need to change that diaper."

"I'm not Andy, I'm Thuperman."

"I don't care who you are, get in here."

He came in, pouting. He looked like Frankie in miniature. Elena had buzz-cut Frankie and Andy's dark hair with her Norelco home barber kit, sparing Mikey because she couldn't bear to touch those pretty blond curls.

She knelt down and undid the pins on either side of Andy's soaked diaper. Along with peeing in it all day he'd done a number two. "You cannot walk around like this. You'll get a rash." She removed the dirty diaper and set it on the toilet lid while she wiped him off.

"I don't care," he said.

She got a clean diaper from a stack on the back of the toilet and pinned a new one on him, then made him step into a plastic diaper cover.

"I don't like that. It pinches my legs."

"Then learn to use the potty and you won't have to wear them anymore," she said, standing up. Andy ran off down the hall.

Elena took the dirty diaper and swished it around in the toilet to get the worst of the poop off before putting it in the diaper bucket. After Angelo left she couldn't afford the diaper service anymore, and had to wash her own, hanging them out to dry on the line behind the house. When the red diaper delivery truck came around the circle twice a week, with its roof-rack full of pristine cotton, she hid indoors, her envy palpable. Her whole house smelled like a diaper bucket. Like poop and pee and sandwich crusts left under the couch and boys' smelly sneakers and blobs of toothpaste left in the sink.

She retrieved Gordie from his playpen and sat down on the couch where she could put her feet up, with Gordie on her lap. Her ankles were swollen from standing all day. Red and purple spider veins smeared the backs of her knees. That's what you got with four kids. Five. There had been another child, between Frankie and Mikey, a little girl they'd named Freda. She had a hole in her heart and had only lived two days, the pressure of her grip almost imperceptible around Elena's little finger.

Elena put her nose down and breathed in Gordie's baby

smells, Johnson's baby shampoo and sour milk from something that had spilled and dried on his pajamas. Her babies each had a unique smell. She could have picked out any one of them in a crowd, blindfolded.

Frankie and Mikey came in with a clamor and turned on the TV. The phone in the kitchen rang. Elena set Gordie on the floor near his brothers and went to answer it. It was Patsy Robbins, the mother of a little boy named Chase that Elena's boys played with around the circle.

"Chase came home saying bad words. He says he learned them from Frankie and Mikey," Patsy said.

"What words?" Elena asked.

"Mucka-fucka-shit-ball," Patsy said. "Not the words I expected from my eight-year-old. I had to wash his mouth out with soap."

Elena wished she could defend her boys, but she was sure they were guilty as charged. "I'm very sorry. I'll have a talk with them."

She hung up and went back into the living room where the boys sprawled on the floor. She turned off the television.

"What'd you do that for?" Frankie said.

"Because Mrs. Robbins just called to tell me that you and Mikey were teaching Chase dirty words."

"Not us," Frankie said.

"What words?" Andy asked.

Elena bent down and pressed her hands over Andy's ears. "Mucka-fucka-shit-ball," she said to Frankie and Mikey, enunciating. "Sound familiar?" She took her hands off Andy's ears.

"Chase couldn't even say it right," Mikey said.

"Shut up, Mikey," Frankie said.

"You cannot teach curse words to the little kids. I shouldn't have to tell you that. And I don't want to hear language like that from you, either. No more TV today."

"That's not fair!" Frankie said, standing up. "Dad says that stuff all the time!"

"Oh, and that makes it right?"

Frankie crossed his arms. "Maybe I'll go live with him," he said.

"Why don't you do that, Frankie. Then you can use that potty mouth all the time."

"I will, then," he said, heading for his room.

"Fine," she called after him. "You just have to find him first." Frankie slammed his door.

Elena wished Angelo were here, so she could slap his face. He had moved them to Tonola Falls so he could take a job supervising the school's physical plant, then as soon as Gordie was born he'd left her in this isolated stink hole, the son-of-a-bitch, with no way to save up enough money to get out, back to New York. If she really wanted to get back to New York. Four boys in a big city, not good. They were better off here, where the amount of trouble they could get into was limited by how far they could ride on their decrepit bike, and there were dozens of adult eyes on them to keep them straight.

Gordie started to cry. She picked him up. He tugged his left ear, twisting it. Another earache. Loud music boomed from the room Frankie shared with Mikey. Frankie blasting his stereo, just to get her goat. She didn't have the energy to do anything about it. She found herself thinking about Rob Whitaker, his last moments, whether he had time to be afraid before he died. Helicopter rotors choked off in mid-air, the sick feeling of something that heavy falling. She buried her nose in Gordie's hair to make the thoughts go away.

The school rented buses to take whoever wanted to go to Rob Whitaker's memorial service, to be held in his hometown just north of Atlanta. Elena talked Mrs. Hensley into staying with the two youngest for the five hours it would take to go to the service and back. She should have taken Frankie and Mikey with her but the challenge of getting them both dressed in their suits and ready to go seemed insurmountable, not to mention making them behave on the bus and during the funeral.

She collared them before she left. "It's a beautiful day. Put your coats on and play outside while I'm gone, and don't do anything dangerous. I told Mrs. Hensley not to let you in except for lunch or to use the bathroom. If you're good, I'll take you to see *Butch Cassidy and the Sundance Kid* next weekend. If I get a bad report, I swear to God, I'll beat the hell out of both of you. I'm not kidding."

The bus ride was heaven. No little boys fighting with each other, the sky outside a bright blue that brought every leaf and blade of grass into sharp focus. When they arrived at the church, there were so many people they couldn't all fit into the building. Since she hadn't been a close friend, Elena stayed outside on the front steps, shoulder to shoulder with others who had come to pay their respects, all standing quiet, straining to hear. Through the church's open double doors Elena could see a framed photo on top of the coffin, of Rob in his dress uniform, looking like a baby. She caught every few words the minister said, valor and bravery and sacrifice, as if dying young was what it took to be a hero.

The burial was in the cemetery behind the church, where tall hemlock trees blocked the sun, their exposed roots skewing some of the older gravestones. Elena pulled her coat more tightly around her and moved with the crowd to where she could see. Rob's parents sat in folding chairs under the shelter the funeral home had set up. His mother cradled a folded flag, listening to the priest, or not listening.

For none of us liveth to himself
and no man dieth to himself.

On a Saturday last spring, not long after Elena had moved with the boys into faculty housing, she had come home from the grocery store with Gordie to find the kitchen even more of a mess than usual. The counter covered with lemon and orange halves with the juice squeezed out, spilled sugar crunching on the floor. She put Gordie in his crib and stormed outside and around the circle looking for the boys so she could jerk a knot in them. When she rounded the curve in front of the boy's dorm, she stopped. Frankie, Mikey, and Andy had set up shop on the steps with her nice glass pitcher and a stack of Dixie cups, and a sign that said "Lemon-Orange-Aid 25 cents." Rob Whitaker was perched on his ten-speed racing bike in front of the boys. As Elena watched he dug in his pocket and pulled out two dollar bills. "Keep the change," he said.

"Wow, thanks, man," Frankie said. Mikey picked up the pitcher and carefully poured Rob a cup of their concoction.

"I always wanted to have a lemonade stand, but my neighborhood didn't get any traffic," Rob said, taking the cup Mikey offered. He emptied it with one gulp. "Excellent." He handed the cup back to Mikey and pushed off on his bike.

"Come again thoon!" Andy yelled. The boys huddled, counting their money.

Rob's kindness had taken the fire out of Elena. Instead of yelling at her boys, she had turned around and gone home.

The priest had finished speaking and men moved forward to lower Rob's casket. Elena looked around her at the people nearby, the tips of their ears turning pink from standing in the cold too long, the sharp heels of the women's shoes sinking into earth.

Off from the crowd a woman stood alone, weeping openly. She was in her forties, silver strands in her black hair, an aunt perhaps. Her thin body sagged against the sky as she keened into air. Without meaning to, Elena raised her right hand and traced the elongated zigzag of the woman's shape, the torso leaning slightly forward, the knees bending in abject grief.

Back at home, Frankie and Mikey were ready to be allowed back into the house. The boys got their Hot Wheels out and began racing them, banging them into the living room wall as hard as they could. Elena started supper. Someone knocked on the kitchen door and she opened it. It was Betty McAfee, the mother Elena liked least on the circle. Betty was one of those ultra-religious protestants there were so many of in this part of Georgia. She was always after Elena to take the boys to her church. Elena didn't go to church because the nearest Catholic church was fifty miles away, and as lapsed a Catholic as she was, she couldn't bring herself to take her kids to a Protestant church.

Betty held something out to Elena, a large paperback book or magazine, pinching it with two fingers as if she didn't want to touch it. "Your Frankie," she said, "spent his day charging the children in the neighborhood fifty cents a peek to look at this."

Elena took the book.

"It's pornography. Disgusting," Betty said. "My Duncan was shocked. He's at home in bed with a sick headache."

Betty's son Duncan was two years older than Frankie and the neighborhood bully. Elena had a hard time imagining him in bed with a headache.

"You've got to do something, Elena. Without a father, those boys need direction more than ever. We have a new youth minister at our church who could do wonders with them."

"I'll talk to Frankie," Elena said, closing the door before Betty could wedge her way in.

Elena looked more closely at the book. It was some kind of adult comic book, drawn in black and white. Most of the pictures were just topless women, but the centerfold showed a well-endowed, naked woman standing waist-deep in a creek, getting screwed by a cattail plant, and apparently enjoying it.

"Frances Anthony Domiano!" Her yell was loud enough to bring all three boys into the kitchen.

She waved the comic book in Frankie's face. "I can't leave you for one day without you doing something like this?"

"What?" Frankie said, in a half-hearted attempt to play innocent.

"This is disgusting, Frankie. And you showed it to younger kids too?"

"It made my dick feel all tingly," Mikey said, grinning.

"Oh, Jesus," Elena said.

"Shut *up*, Mikey," Frankie said, hitting Mikey on the arm.

Elena smacked Frankie on the shoulder with the comic book. "Where did you get this?"

"Duncan found it in the dumpster behind the Victory Home."

"And then you and Duncan decided to share it with the whole neighborhood? And charge admission?"

"It was his idea," Frankie said. Elena didn't doubt it, though Duncan's mother would never believe her perfect son would do such a thing.

"Where's the money you made? Hand it over."

"Duncan has it. He said he'd go halvsies but he took it all home with him."

Elena closed her eyes. How was she supposed to handle this situation? She didn't know what to do with a pubescent boy. Her family had been all girls. She understood Frankie being curious, but charging admission, geez. Where was that bastard Angelo when she needed him?

She opened her eyes and ripped the centerfold out of the comic book. "Real women don't look like this, you know. If you think this is real, you'll never recognize it when you find the real thing."

"I know," Frankie muttered. He looked down at his feet, his face red. At least he had the decency to be ashamed.

"You're grounded," she said. "For a week. Come straight home from school and go to your room."

She herded the boys out of the kitchen and tore up the rest of the comic book, dumping the pieces in the garbage and covering them with coffee grounds so Frankie wouldn't be tempted to dig them out. She could feel a tension headache starting at the base of her skull. Outside the kitchen window the sky was pitch black. Her cooking had fogged up the window. Elena reached up a finger and drew on the pane, trying to capture the lines of the woman she had seen at Rob Whitaker's funeral, a slant down, then the knees slightly bent. Her finger squeaked along the glass.

The week after Thanksgiving, the senior class installed a bench in front of the administration building in Rob Whitaker's honor and the headmaster handed out Christmas bonuses to the cafeteria workers. Elena had been saving to buy Frankie the bike he wanted, a five-speed Schwinn Stingray, with a long, sloping seat and hand brakes. He had outgrown the rattly bike he shared with Mikey. His knees came up almost to his ears when he rode it.

The cafeteria manager gave her an hour off during the morning and she drove to the hardware store in Clarksville to buy the bike. The store owner rolled it out and fit it into her trunk. The bike was a beauty, the iridescent green of a bottle fly. She took it to the school librarian's house to hide until Christmas.

That evening Frankie told her he needed three dollars for a field trip, and she sent him to get it out of her purse in her bedroom. Gordie was cranky, no doubt coming down with something. She carried him into her bedroom to put him in his crib. Frankie sat on her bed with her purse on his lap. He was holding the hardware store receipt for the bike. When he saw her, he shoved it back into her purse.

Elena put Gordie in his crib and then turned toward Frankie. His face was bright with the excitement of knowing what he was going to get. Lit up like that, he was almost as beautiful as Mikey. She picked up her purse and moved it to the dresser without saying a word. She was glad he knew, proud that she'd been able to buy the bike for him. It felt like a thumb to the nose at her no-good husband, who didn't send her any money for the kids. The next time Angelo called to talk to Frankie, if he ever did, Frankie could brag to him about it.

Gordie got sick. He grew worse over the next couple of days, coughing and sputtering in his crib while Elena lay rigid in her bed with her eyes wide open, terrified he would stop breathing. It got so bad that on the third morning Mrs. Hensley called Elena at work to come and take him to the doctor.

"It's asthma," the doctor said. "You'll need to get a nebulizer and neb him twice a day. I'll write you the prescription." When

Elena asked him how much the nebulizer and medicine would cost, his answer made her sick.

Back at home she called her mother-in-law in New York to see if she knew where Angelo was. Angelo had never gone a week without talking to his mother, but the old bat acted like she hadn't heard from him.

"Tell him the baby's sick," Elena said. "Tell him I need money for medicine. Tell him to be a man." She waited by the phone but Angelo didn't call. Finally, an hour before the older boys were due home from school, Elena bundled Gordie up. She left Andy with Mrs. Hensley and drove to the school librarian's house, where she wheeled Frankie's bike out of the crawl space under the house, wrestled it into her car and drove to Clarksville.

When she got home, Mrs. Hensley had left and the boys were playing Rock'em Sock'em Robots in the living room. Elena set up the nebulizer on the kitchen table and nebbed Gordie for the first time. It seemed to ease his breathing. She took him to her bedroom and put him in his crib, then called Frankie in.

"I need to talk to you about Christmas," she said. She sat him down on the bed and sat next to him. "I know you found the receipt."

He started to deny it, then stopped. He looked so happy.

"I had to take it back," she said. "To pay for Gordie's medicine and the nebulizer. If I can save some more money I'll buy you the bike in the spring."

She watched the brightness fade from Frankie's face. He lowered his head, squeezing his eyes shut, and started to cry.

Elena put a hand on the back of his neck. "You're too old to cry about it," she said gently.

"I know," he said, crying harder.

Gordie whimpered in his crib. Without her asking him to, Frankie went to the crib, still crying. He checked Gordie's diaper and reached for a clean one, wiping his eyes with it before he folded it the way she had taught him and began to change his little brother.

Elena walked out onto the front porch. She stood there in the cold. Across campus, Christmas lights shone from the windows of the administration building. Soon the students would leave for the holidays and go home to their comfortable houses, where everything they had asked for would wait for them under the tree. Except at Rob Whitaker's house, where his parents wouldn't have the heart to decorate, and at the home of the woman Elena had seen at Rob's funeral, who would sit alone at her kitchen table and shut her eyes tight to make the holiday pass.

Dead leaves blew across the porch. Inside, Mikey and Andy started to fight, the thump and roll of their bodies making the house shake, until Frankie yelled at them to cut it out. Elena let her knees bend and leaned forward slightly, fitting her body into the shape she remembered, until she became the weeping woman. She held on to the porch rail and cried, in a way that she hadn't when her husband left or her little daughter died. Because of Frankie's bike, and because Rob Whitaker had been a good boy, and Elena knew how hard it was to raise a good boy.

Things Summoned

The girl, Lorna, likes to run away. She gathers things: Snack Pack puddings saved from her lunches, a rusty can opener, a stack of Tupperware cups. If you asked her she would tell you it was this collecting of items that drew her away from home, not any unhappiness. She likes the packing, the planning, her spot in the woods, the quiet, all hers to imagine in.

Her hiding place is a quarter mile into the woods behind her house, across a creek where water tricks over round brown stones. An old door bridges the creek. On the other side is the place she calls the Rocky Mountains. Boulders jut out of the ground in a circle of blunted teeth. She can perch on them or use the open space at their center as a campsite. When she sits on top of the biggest one, its surface warm or cold depending on the weather, she feels magnetized to the mountain. She knows how ancient it is. She builds it little pebble houses, imagining the tickle the mountain feels each time she adds another breath of weight.

She transports her supplies across the creek bridge in an old doll carriage she played with when she was small. A shallow cave has eroded in the red clay at the base of one leaning boulder and she puts her things in it so they will stay dry if it rains. She keeps a notebook of the sky there, each day logging what it looks like. She is certain a pattern will emerge, that she will become a Predictor of the Sky. This day, the sky is the blue of a puzzle piece and she carefully records it before she puts the notebook away and rolls the doll carriage back through the woods to her house.

The girl's mother, Sarah, watches from the kitchen window as Lorna emerges from the woods. Sarah knows where Lorna goes. They used to go there together, when Lorna was still small enough for Sarah to lift her up onto the rocks. They invited fairies for tea, serving creek water in pink plastic teacups, mud pies, cookies made from bits of bark. On a blustery day when their fairy feast blew away, Lorna reached up to touch Sarah's cheek and said, "Mama, you hair is windy." In those days, Sarah knew before Lorna did when Lorna was hungry or sad, when the covers had shifted in the crib leaving an arm exposed to the cold. They might as well have been one person. Now, Lorna calls Sarah *Mom*. Lorna's independence leaves Sarah lonely. She is afraid to ask Lorna what she remembers. If Lorna no longer believes in fairies, Sarah doesn't want to know.

Lorna leaves the doll buggy at the bottom of the back porch stairs and goes inside to the kitchen where her mother stands at the sink. Her father comes in and begins opening and closing drawers, looking for something. The kitchen's overhead light glares off his bald spot. Her mother crosses her arms, watching him.

"I bought a brand-new roll of Scotch tape just last week, and it's not where I left it," her father says.

"I haven't used your tape," her mother says.

"We need to keep this house more organized."

Keeping the house in order is her mother's job, and her mother's eyes narrow into slits.

The reason her father can't find the tape is that Lorna transported it to her campsite the day before. She thought she might need it for repairing things. She will have to bring it back to stop the seething that swirls around the kitchen.

"Have you done your homework, Lorna?" Her father, the headmaster, expects his daughter to study.

"I'll do it now." Lorna goes to her room. She closes the door and spreads her homework on her bed. She can hear her parents' muffled voices, rising in spikes like the bark of dogs. She wonders what would happen if she were at the Rocky Mountains and a pack of dogs appeared, how she would defend herself. She is wearing her favorite hooded sweatshirt and decides she would pull the hood over her head and curl into a ball. To practice, she does just that, burying her face in her pillow, arms around her head, elbows pressed to her ears. The dogs are close, paws on her back, breath whistling. She cannot breathe.

The bedroom door opens and her mother comes in with a basket of clothes to put away. "Lorna?"

Lorna remembers that there are no dogs and that she is free to lift her head. She sits up in bed, sucking air into her lungs.

Her mother frowns. "What's wrong, honey?"

"Nothing," Lorna says, though she has almost smothered herself with her pillow.

Sarah shifts the laundry basket to her hip and searches Lorna's face. Their faces are alike, high cheekbones, wide-set eyes, lips that will never need cosmetics for color. With age Lorna's features will stretch into Sarah's same beauty. Only Lorna's jaw is different. It is her father's jaw. Sarah tries not to resent it.

At the Rocky Mountains the next afternoon Lorna sits on top of the biggest boulder, tracing its streaks of orange and gray and black. She knows the types of rock: igneous, sedimentary, and metamorphic pressurized by the ball of heat at the center of the earth. This time of year, when the foliage has died back, she can see the lines where the mountain folded over on itself. On her lap is the store-bought rock collection her father gave her for Christmas, a plastic case with partitions separating quartz, agate, red and yellow ochre, a lazurite crystal, obsidian, blue calcite, a tiny chip of sapphire. Her father has told her that all the rocks in the collection came from within fifty miles of their house in Tonola Falls. Others just like them are in this mountain somewhere. She can feel them below the surface, little points of light. She takes the rocks out of the case one by one and sets them on the boulder's surface so that each domesticated stone can call out to its wild kin through the veins in the rock, luring them to the surface where she can pluck them.

A raindrop hits her cheek and another spatters on the plastic case. Lorna wipes her face. Her mother emerges from the direction of the creek, calling to her.

"Didn't you hear the thunder?" her mother says when she reaches Lorna. "Didn't you see the clouds?"

Lorna has seen the clouds, spreading like an angry purple birthmark across the face of the sky. She logged them in her notebook, now tucked out of sight.

"Honestly, Lorna, you've got to watch the daydreaming." Her mother helps her put her rock collection back in its case. Lorna starts to wheel the empty baby carriage toward the creek. The rain comes harder now, tapping on the vinyl of the carriage. Her mother grabs the carriage and hefts it over her shoulder to carry it across the creek, balancing gracefully on the wobbly bridge. Lorna follows her. They get to their house just as the heavens open up.

When the rain stops Lorna and her mother drive up to the Point for groceries and gas. The trading post sits on the edge of the gorge. The owner's slow, small-eyed daughter sells boiled peanuts from the parking lot. The owner, Mr. Jarret, pumps their gas. "Be sure to keep your doors locked," he says. "Somebody jimmied the lock on my peanut stand last night and walked off with a sack of peanuts, and two vacation homes down at the lake have been broken into." While he and her mother talk, Lorna examines the drowned earthworms that sprawl across the blacktop. The parking lot is full of puddles. She steps to the edge of the biggest one. Oil forms a rainbow sheen on the surface so that she can't see the bottom, only her own reflection. She imagines the puddle deep enough to go through to China. Girls in coned straw hats lift their knees to step through rice paddies. Fishermen use loons with banded necks to catch fish. Lorna is teetering on the edge, about to fall to the other side of the world, when her mother speaks. "Lorna, did you hear me? We're going inside."

Lorna blinks. A peanut shell floats like a rattan boat in the puddle.

Her mother puts a hand on the back of her head and leads her into the store. Boards squeak under their feet. Mr. Jarret has built a deck off the back where the tourists who come in summer can put a quarter in a telescope to look at the gorge. Lorna goes and plays with the telescope, but without a coin her eye is blind and the wind bites too fiercely to stay outside. She trails after her mother to the checkout line, near a rack of candy and gum. She has convinced herself that anything that falls from the rack is free. A roll of Life Savers has fallen and rolled. As her mother pays, Lorna picks it up and puts it in her pocket.

Back at home, her mother fingers the rat's nest that has formed at the base of Lorna's skull. "How about I wash your hair and French braid it? I'll make hot chocolate. Just us girls."

"I can't right now," Lorna says. She wants to take the Life Savers to her secret place. She feels her mother watching her as she walks into the woods.

The sky the next day is the dull white of a blank stare as far as Lorna's eyes can follow it. At the campsite the ground is frozen hard. She goes to the little cave where she stores her provisions. She reaches for the Life Savers, then stops. Someone has opened them. The first two candies are gone, cherry and pineapple if she goes by the wrapper. Whoever took them has folded the waxed paper down carefully, as if they wanted to be polite even in their hunger.

She looks around. There is no other sign that anyone but her has been there. She imagines a fairy friend, a girl like her only in miniature, her step too light to leave tracks. Lorna tears a page from her sky notebook and writes a note. "You are welcome to more." She tucks it under the Life Savers.

She walks back over the creek and through the woods, past her house and across campus to the school library. She needs to know more about fairies and other woodland creatures. She pulls what books she can find from the shelves. The school librarian, Miss Evelyn, finds her kneeling in the stacks.

"Anything I can help you with?" The skin of Miss Evelyn's

face is crisscrossed with wrinkles, like a piece of paper that has been balled up and then smoothed out again.

"I was looking up fairies," Lorna says.

"Fairy tales?"

"No, stuff about them," Lorna says.

Miss Evelyn crouches beside her, flipping through the books on the shelf. "What was it you wanted to know?"

"What they eat," Lorna says.

Miss Evelyn's fingers pause on the spine of a book. She looks at Lorna.

Lorna once stole the first green pepper of the season from Miss Evelyn's garden. She hadn't meant to, but when she passed by there it was, waxy and perfect though not yet fully grown. She had ducked across the garden rows, picked it and run and was already hidden in the woods by the time the librarian came yelling out of her house. Lorna stashed the pepper at her camp-site, planning to eat it later, but when she returned ants had devoured it and it was wasted.

"I'll just take these," Lorna says, gathering her books.

Miss Evelyn stands up, knees cracking. At the circulation desk Lorna pulls cards from the pockets in the back of the books and writes her name in cursive.

"Let me know what you learn," Miss Evelyn says.

Miss Evelyn watches Lorna leave. She files the cards away. Something doesn't feel right to Miss Evelyn. She has lived a long time in the world and among her books. She knows the danger of things summoned from imagination.

Lorna decides to run an experiment to determine what sort of creature her friend is. She will set out a selection of foods. The food taken will tell her who is visiting her campsite. She barters with her friend Chase for some of the old army C-rations he found. It costs her dearly—her Magic Eight Ball and a pair of American Airlines wings her grandmother got on a flight from Pennsylvania. She sets the C-rations out in a line with a Slim Jim, three cinnamon toothpicks, some dry dog food, and flower petals she pinched from an impatiens her mother has brought inside for the winter. She hopes it will be the flower petals, fairy food, that get eaten.

The next day when she returns to the Rocky Mountains, the ground is black where someone has lit a campfire and then let it burn out. A package of stew from the C-rations is torn open but uneaten, the contents oozing out onto the ground. The stew is two wars old and Lorna does not blame her friend for not eating it. The Slim Jim is gone, the wrapper lying on the ground among flower petals and scattered toothpicks. Ants crawl over pieces of dog food. Her friend is human, perhaps a girl her age whose parents have died and who must live on her own like the Boxcar Children.

Lorna looks around the campsite. The things she keeps in the hollow at the base of the rock have been moved around. Her notebook is open. Her friend has been reading her journal of the sky.

Lorna takes the notebook and turns to a clean page. She writes, "If you are reading this, please tell me who you are. I want to be friends." She leaves the notebook in the hollow with her note showing.

On Saturday it snows, just enough to dust the ground. Lorna's mother is in the kitchen in a fluffy robe, making pancakes in the shape of Mickey Mouse and humming "Raindrops Keep Falling on My Head." Her father drinks coffee and reads the paper. When the pancakes are ready her mother puts them on the table and sits down.

"How about a pedicure this morning, Lorna?" Her mother wiggles her own pretty toes. "My *Cosmo* has an article about how to do it professionally. You can pick any color polish you want, even my bright red."

Her father lowers his paper and looks over his glasses, first at her mother, then at the pans weeping pancake batter into the sink.

"What?" her mother says.

"Are you going to leave those dishes?"

"You could do them," her mother says.

"I work all week," he says.

"They'll keep," her mother says. "What do you say, Lorna?"

Lorna doesn't want to hurt her mother's feelings but she is eager to get to her place and see if her friend has left a return note. "I kind of want to go out in the snow." She sees that her answer has cost her mother a victory of sorts and she is sorry, but her friend is waiting for her.

She gets dressed and goes outside. The sky is the smudgy gray of dirty fingerprints around a light switch. Skeleton trees striped with snow scrape against it. She heads into the woods. At the creek, the door that serves as a bridge is broken, split down the middle as if by some giant foot. The two halves lie in the water. She wades the creek in her sneakers, the cold taking her breath away.

When she gets close to her rocks, she finds peanut shells strewn over the ground. She follows their trail among the boulders, to where her friend made the fire. Snow has covered the fire's ashes. In the snow are footprints, big and booted, walking all over each other.

She hears a rustle of paper and looks up. A man is there, standing on an incline a few feet away. He holds her journal in his hands.

The man is dressed in soldier green and camouflage. He is younger than her parents but older than the high school boys her father teaches. The bill of his cap shadows his eyes and his coat hangs from his bones. He has been bigger than he is now.

Lorna knows her propensity to imagine things and she tries to de-imagine him, but he is real and does not disappear. She grasps at the manners her parents have taught her. "My name's Lorna. What's yours?" Her voice trembles, weak in the still air.

"Benson," he says. His lips barely move. The voice seems to come from a cave.

The man is broken, Lorna can feel it, the bridge between his mind and heart split completely like the board across the creek.

She reaches behind her and touches the nearest boulder. The mountain's heartbeat pulses in her fingertips. Fear melts down her body and legs, into the thin covering of snow and the dead winter grass beneath it. It penetrates hard clay and runs into the veins of the mountain that spreads under Lorna and the man and out, all the way to the house where her mother sits painting her toes. *Mama, come get me.*

Sarah sits with her foot propped up, cotton between her toes and a magazine open beside her. She has finished with one foot and is about to paint the first stroke of pink on the other when she feels her daughter's fear enter her body and push upward to her heart. Her hand lurches, smearing nail polish. The fear squeezes the back of her neck and she is up and out the door, magazine in hand, rolling it into a hard baton as she goes. "Lorna!"

She runs through the woods, her bare feet pounding a wild drumbeat in the snow. Her long hair streams behind her, collecting twigs and leaves. She leaps the creek and breaks into the circle of rocks with the snarl of an animal. The man is standing in front of Lorna, about to take a step forward. Sarah lunges at him, jabbing the magazine in his face. "*Back off!*"

Lorna sees the man's eyes focus. He holds up his palms. "Whoa, lady." He is no longer hypnotized the way he was before. He is awake now.

Her mother grabs Lorna and pushes her, running, toward the creek. Lorna listens for the man's footsteps on the hard ground behind them but he doesn't follow. Her mother has her by the arm. "*Run. Run.*" They burst out of the woods and into their own yard, up the steps and inside. Her mother slams the door and locks it.

Lorna's father stands in the kitchen, startled.

"Call the police," her mother says, and for once her father does not argue. He is on the phone and dialing.

Lorna's mother takes her to the living room and sits her down. She pulls off Lorna's wet sneakers and socks and rubs her cold feet. The two of them sit pressed together on the couch with their knees drawn up. Her mother's feet are bloody. The new polish on her nails has smeared into hard pink waves. Lorna reaches out a finger to touch.

Twilight Song

Strong Louisiana sun warms nine-year-old Margaret's closed eyelids. A ceiling fan turns above her head and a man's voice calls her name gently from the next room. She lies still. She is playing hide and seek with Boudreaux, the prisoner who serves as her family's manservant and nanny. Her sickly mother objects to Boudreaux but Margaret's father, the warden of Angola Prison, trusts the prisoner above all men. Margaret loves Boudreaux. Where her parents are distant, he is kind. He plays with her, letting her choose the rules of the games, pulling curly gray Spanish moss down from trees in the yard to make beards for them both, picking her up when she falls, and dancing her across the long covered porch, singing to comfort her. With her arms around his neck she can feel the songs vibrate in his throat. The words are sometimes English, sometimes French, always just for her.

She has found the perfect hiding place today, under the rumpled sheets of her own unmade bed. Her bedroom is just off the porch and she hears Boudreaux go outside, his sandals whispering. He is hunting in the wrong direction. She giggles, keeping her eyes closed. His voice, still coaxing, grows fainter as he walks across the porch and down into the lower part of the yard, toward the sugar cane field that separates the warden's house from the low, whitewashed camp buildings of the prison. A breeze has blown all morning and Margaret imagines it lifting Boudreaux's dark hair and then moving on into the field, parting the growing cane like some fast-moving underground animal.

She can no longer hear Boudreaux and her nose is beginning to itch. She opens her eyes, ready to throw off the sheet and run after him, ending the game, but she freezes. Someone is next to her in the bed. An arm lies on top of the sheet, nestled in the white folds of cloth to her right. It is an old woman's arm, dark patches flecking the back of the hand, clusters of tiny purple veins under the skin, a red crack chapped into the first knuckle. Margaret holds her breath, afraid to move, afraid to call Boudreaux. The arm is still. She doesn't know if its owner is alive or dead. She wants to scream but she can't make a sound.

"That's right, hon. Open those eyes for me." A face looms over her, smiling, a white cap bobby-pinned to salt-and-pepper hair. "I'm Nanette, your nurse. I just need to get you turned. It's not good to lie in one position too long." The woman slips strong arms under Margaret and rolls her onto her left side. The arm, the old woman's arm, flops across Margaret's body. She tries again to scream but her voice won't work.

The woman comes around to the other side of the bed and sees Margaret's terror. "Oh, now. Don't you be anxious, hon. You've had a stroke. You're in the hospital and we're taking good care of you." She lifts the arm and places it gently on the sheet near Margaret's chest, palm facing down. Margaret understands now. The arm is hers.

She closes her eyes. The sun is still warm on her face. She stands on the porch, wood smooth under her bare feet. Boudreaux is in the yard, calling calmly for her, not yet worried that he hasn't found her. He sees her and waves, a wide smile on his face. "You win the game, *cher.*"

She runs down to him, throwing her arms around his waist and holding tight. "Boudreaux! I was so scared!"

He stoops to hug her. Straight black hairs stand out on his muscled arms. He smells of the biscuits he baked for her that morning. "What's all this? Who's scaring my girl?"

Margaret can't explain.

"Let's have us a dance, make you forget all about it." Boudreaux holds her hands and she steps up onto his sandaled feet. They do a slow two-step around the yard and Boudreaux sings her a song.

In the twilight of my years, *cher*
My dim eyes will see you clearly,
My deaf ears will hear your sweet voice.
Now while we are still young,
Turn for me, turn for me on the floor,
Dansons, dansons, dansons.

The breeze brings the smell of cane juice boiling down to sugar at the prison's refinery. Beyond Boudreaux, prisoners as small as Margaret's thumb work on the levees that keep the Mississippi River from rushing in and flooding Angola and all of West Feliciana Parish. The noon dinner bell from the prison clangs in the distance and she hears muffled horse's hooves as her father arrives home to eat his lunch, but Boudreaux hums on.

The next time Margaret wakes up, Evelyn is there, in a chair by the hospital bed, reading a book. Margaret almost weeps with relief. Evelyn's short hair is silver-gray, her brown eyes still piercing though their whites have yellowed. Her face is tanned and furrowed from years in her garden. Lines laugh upward from her mouth.

Evelyn sees that she is awake and puts her book down with a smile. "There you are." She takes Margaret's hands in hers. Margaret can feel the warmth of Evelyn's skin on her left hand but not her right. Evelyn answers the questions Margaret cannot articulate. "You've been here two days. You went to bed with a bad headache and then I found you on the floor with one side of your face drooping. You scared me to death."

Margaret tries to apologize but all that comes out is an ugly grunt.

"Don't worry about talking. It'll come. They're going to move you to a rehabilitation hospital in a couple of days and work on it with you." Evelyn squeezes Margaret's good hand. "You know I can talk enough for both of us."

A heavyset woman enters the room. "How are we today? I'm Trudy, your physical therapist. Let's get you sitting up and see what you can do." She and Evelyn help Margaret sit up, propping her back with pillows. The therapist takes Margaret's flaccid arm and begins to rotate it. "I'm exercising your muscles. Pretty soon you'll be able to do this for yourself." When she finishes with the arm she does the same thing to Margaret's right leg. Margaret has more feeling in the leg than in the arm and can even move it a little bit herself. "Look at that," the therapist says. "I believe you're ready to try transferring from the bed to that toilet seat." She points to a toilet chair by the bed.

They take it slow. The therapist helps her get both legs over the side of the bed and shows her how to place her good hand on the rail of the toilet chair before pushing herself up off the bed. "You're a little thing, aren't you? Hardly weigh anything."

Margaret puts most of her weight on her good leg. She can feel Evelyn behind her, holding herself back from helping. Margaret gets turned and sits down with relief on the toilet seat.

"I never thought I'd be so proud to see you make it to the john," Evelyn says.

Evelyn was the one thing Margaret had to thank Jack Frazier for. Margaret was twenty-two, newly graduated from the music conservatory at Baton Rouge, when she met Jack. She was in New Orleans interviewing for a position as voice teacher at Madame Fournier's Select Seminary for Young Ladies, a job her parents approved of to fill the time until she met a suitable man and married. Margaret was a singer, her operatic voice near professional quality. She was the first to acknowledge her limitations, a certain thinness of the notes at the high end of her range no matter how well she controlled her breath or how many exercises she did. It didn't matter, she loved to sing, and she looked forward to teaching other young women to love it as much as she did.

The school occupied an antebellum mansion on a residential street in New Orleans. Its high wrought-iron fence assured parents that their daughters would be safe from the sinfulness that spilled from the bars of the nearby French Quarter. As Margaret approached the front door she noticed wood rot in one of the porch's white columns, the decay so severe a small animal could have set up house in the hollow at the base. She lifted a hand to knock but the door opened, and a young man stepped out, as startled to see her as she was to see him.

"Excuse me," Margaret said. "I have an appointment to see Madame Fournier?"

A slow smile spread across the young man's face. He was handsome, his dark hair slicked back so that every comb stroke showed, blue eyes with lashes as long as a girl's. "Allow me to show you in. I'm Jack Frazier. I teach piano and organ here."

"Margaret Arnoult. How nice to meet you. I'm actually here about the voice teacher position."

"Wonderful!" He stepped aside to let her pass. As she did, he touched her elbow, lightly cupping it to steer her toward a drawing room to the right. An electric jolt shot up Margaret's arm and down to the center of her body. Sheltered for so long, she had never experienced such a feeling. She raised her fingers to the side of her throat and felt her heart jumping.

Jack introduced her to Madame Fournier and Margaret got the job. He began courting her, his touches always just this side of proper, his upper arm rubbing against hers in a crowd, his hand on her back to guide her at every crossroad, finally the kisses and the front of his clothed body pressed against hers, driving her mad. He played for her, long beautiful fingers stroking the piano keys the way they stroked her. She married him in front of a magistrate one Friday afternoon in hurricane season, with witnesses whose names she couldn't decipher on the marriage license.

They found an apartment, living on their teaching salaries and the money Jack made as organist at the Episcopal church. The voice lessons Margaret taught in the afternoons followed Jack's last piano lesson, and sometimes when she stood in the hall outside Madame Fournier's salon she could hear him laughing with his student, a curvaceous brunette named Chloe

Blanchard. When the door opened, the insolent look the girl gave Margaret left her feeling small and colorless.

On a Tuesday morning when Margaret arrived at the school after Jack, she found him and Madame Fournier speaking with raised voices in the drawing room. Chloe Blanchard had complained. The music master had put his hands on her. Her father was threatening to close down the school.

"A schoolgirl crush. She must have been angry that I didn't return her affections," Jack protested. As Margaret entered the room he took her hand, squeezing it hard.

Madame was unmoved. "I must ask you to leave at once. And I have no choice but to inform the rector at All Souls. He won't be able to keep you on as organist. Margaret may continue teaching here, if the parents don't object."

"Like hell," Jack said. "If I leave, Margaret leaves."

"Jack," Margaret said.

"Suit yourself," Madame said.

Jack pushed Margaret ahead of him through the door, across the columned porch, through the iron gate to the street. "That old cow," he seethed.

"Jack, what will we do?" Margaret was horrified. They had no savings, no prospects.

"We'll ask your parents for help. They have money," Jack said.

"I don't know," Margaret said, remembering her father's rigid silence when she telephoned him to tell him she had married. He had refused to put her mother on the line, afraid that her constitution was too weak to take the shock.

"Ask them today," Jack said.

Margaret's room at the rehabilitation hospital is more comfortable, less sterile than her room at the regular hospital. The only thing she hates about it is the large mirror on the wall. She sees herself, unpleasantly thin, the gray roots of her hair grown out, the right side of her body and face still drooping grotesquely like a distortion in a fun house mirror.

They teach her to walk with a walker and to bathe and dress herself with one hand. She has speech therapy and is able to say a few words. Evelyn comes every day. She sits in a chair in the corner out of the therapists' way, quietly cheering Margaret on.

"What is this?" The physical therapist asks the third morning, putting something in Margaret's weak hand. Margaret looks at it. She can see it, but she can't recognize it. She doesn't know what it is. She wants to please. The thing has color. "Red?" She looks over at Evelyn in the corner. Evelyn nods, encouraging her. Margaret is supposed to know what the thing is. She can feel it but not recognize the shape. Even smell it, but can't place the smell.

The therapist gently takes the thing from Margaret and transfers it to her good hand, and Margaret knows what it is. "Ball," she says. She lifts it to her face. The smell is rubber.

"Very good. Don't you fret about it. That happens to people. Your right side will come back to you."

Margaret's father, the retired warden, made the trip from St. Francisville to see them. Margaret cleaned the apartment and put out all of their nicest things, but when her father entered she saw the place as he did—the worn carpet, Jack's piano in the corner crowding the small living room, pigeons doing vulgar things on the window sill. And she saw Jack as her father did, a dandy, perfectly shaved and coiffed, who couldn't support a wife. She introduced them. Her father ignored the hand Jack offered and sniffed the neighbor's cooking smells. He took a seat in the living room and Margaret and Jack perched on the sofa across from him. Her father had grown elderly since Margaret left home. A gray tint underlay his skin. His black suit was shiny with wear.

"Sir, we appreciate you coming," Jack said. "Margaret and I find ourselves in a bind, and just need a little help getting back on our feet."

"Money," her father said. "You want money."

Jack swallowed. "Yes, sir."

"No," her father said.

Jack looked at Margaret and then back at the warden. "Sir, it would only be a loan. We'd pay you back, you have my word."

Her father shook his head. "My wife and I have discussed it. We have very little money to give even if we were so inclined. Our holdings are all still underwater from the last flood, crops all ruined. And we feel the two of you have brought this trouble on yourselves. This *marriage*." He swept an arm toward the pigeons on the windowsill. "Margaret, your mother and I are very disappointed."

Margaret held her eyes open wide to keep tears from spilling out.

Jack stood up. "That's it, then." He walked to the door and opened it, motioning for her father to leave.

At the door her father turned to Margaret. "Goodbye."

"Goodbye," she said.

Her father left and Jack closed the door after him with more force than was necessary. The two of them stood still in the quiet apartment, listening to the muffled cooing of the pigeons outside.

"What are we going to do?" Margaret asked.

When he looked at her, Jack's eyes were cold. "I have a plan," he said. He left the apartment and was gone for hours. When he returned he was drunk, exuding bourbon with every breath, stiff pieces of his normally perfect hair flopping over to the wrong side of his part. He stumbled inside, grabbed the back of the sofa to keep from falling, and pressed papers into her hands.

She looked at the papers. Sheet music. "What is this?"

"Our living," he slurred. "A guy I know owns a club on Dauphine Street. You're going to sing and I'll play the piano."

"But I don't sing this kind of music," Margaret said. She hated jazz, in all its forms. To her classically trained ear it sounded like pots being dropped on a kitchen floor.

He stepped closer, took the sheets of music out of her hand, and set them carefully on the sofa, then pushed her so violently she stumbled backward into his piano. They hadn't been able to afford to have it tuned, and when she fell against it high and low notes sagged together miserably.

"You'll sing it." He went into the bedroom and slammed the door, leaving her sitting bruised on the piano bench. That was the first time he hurt her.

The night of their debut he gripped her arm hard as he led her through the French Quarter. Everything about the place frightened Margaret. The loud music blaring from the bars, the press of bodies, men laughing too loudly on street corners. She imagined they were laughing at her. She wrapped her sweater around herself to hide the clingy red dress Jack had insisted she wear. Its neck was so low that when she put it on, he had been able to reach inside and scoop her breast out, bending to bite her nipple. She was mortified.

The club, Duquesne's, had a cramped, dark room inside and a much larger courtyard bar outside. A piano and low stage for musicians divided the two. The evening was mild and people filled the courtyard. Jack pushed Margaret ahead of him into the bar to look for the owner. Serious drinkers perched at the bar. In the back, two tables of Negro men in white jackets sat smoking. Margaret saw a flash of brass and realized they were the club's jazz orchestra. Some of the men glanced up as they entered, their dark faces uninterested.

Jack led her to an empty table. "Wait here." He was soon laughing at the bar with the club manager, too absorbed even to think to bring her a glass of water. She didn't know what to do with her eyes. She didn't want to look at Jack or the musicians. She turned toward the street, hoping the piano would keep people in the courtyard from seeing her and pitying a woman alone. She closed her eyes, wishing she were invisible.

"We see you back there," a voice said. Chairs scraped and Margaret opened her eyes. Two women sat down at her table. One had bobbed hair and wore a short sleeveless dress like a hundred other women on Dauphine Street that night. The other was dressed in a black tuxedo, with her short brown hair slicked behind her ears and an unlit cigarillo in her hand. But for the breasts that strained against her buttoned tuxedo jacket, Margaret might have mistaken her for a man. "You looked lonely," the tuxedoed woman said.

"Evelyn here can't bear to see anyone lonely, and neither can I," the other woman said. "We're determined to keep you company." She held out a delicate hand for Margaret to shake. "I'm Adelicia Hughes, and this is my cousin, Evelyn Craig."

Margaret shook Aldelicia's soft hand, then Evelyn's warm dry one. Margaret could feel calluses on Evelyn's palm. "I'm Margaret," she said.

"Margaret, not to pry, but you don't seem to be enjoying yourself," Adelicia said.

"I'm just nervous, I suppose. I have to sing shortly," Margaret said.

"You're a singer! Well, I am in cultured company tonight. Evelyn here is a novelist," said Adelicia.

Margaret looked at Evelyn. "Are you? Any titles I would know?"

Evelyn smiled. "Probably not."

"Evelyn's novel is what we call *racy*," Adelicia said. "Not available in your local public library. Our common grandmother would be scandalized." She looked around. "There's a sorry lack of waiters in this place. I'm going to the bar. What can I bring you ladies?"

"Gin and tonic," Evelyn said.

"Water would be lovely, thank you," Margaret said.

Adelicia went to the bar and was soon chatting with Jack and the other men.

"Do you sing here regularly?" Evelyn asked.

"Tonight's my first time."

"With the band?"

"No, my husband." Margaret pointed to Jack, who had his arm around Adelicia's shoulder. "He plays piano."

"Don't mind Adelicia," Evelyn said.

Margaret pressed her lips together until they hurt.

Adelicia sashayed back to their table clutching three glasses in a triangle. Jack was right behind her. Adelicia put the drinks on the table and Margaret reached for the water but Jack stopped her. "We're up."

On the low stage Margaret stood in front of the microphone and Jack started to play a fast number. "Act like you're having fun," he had said when they practiced. Margaret did her best, snapping her fingers and moving her shoulders to the beat, trying to fit all the words in without falling behind Jack. Most of the patrons treated them as background noise, though a few tables of rowdy young men near the front were paying more attention than Margaret liked, stomping their feet and whooping their approval. As she jiggled through the song, she could feel her dress slipping down her shoulders, the neckline gaping wider.

"That's right, baby! Let 'em pop right outta there!" a man on the front row yelled. Heads turned toward Margaret. She pulled the two sides of her plunging neckline together to try to hide her cleavage, still singing.

"Aw, don't tease, honey! Show 'em to us again!"

Margaret suddenly could not remember the words to the song. In desperation she started to scat, the way Jack had taught her that week, hating the nonsense sounds that came out of her mouth. Jack glared at her from the piano, but no one else noticed. The number seemed to go on forever. Margaret wished the stage would open up and let her fall through. She remembered a trick her voice professor at the Conservatory had taught her for nerves, a pressure point in the center of the palm that she could press with the thumb of her other hand to stop any trembling of the voice or knees while she sang. She tried it now, digging her thumb into her skin as hard as a crucifixion nail, with no relief. Out in the audience the drunk men had lost interest. At a table to their right Evelyn Craig sat alone, watching Margaret, a slight smile on her face.

When their set was over the jazz orchestra took over. Margaret slipped past Jack before he could waylay her. She found the bar's back door and went out, into a quiet alley where the air didn't smell of cigarettes and spilled liquor. Hands shaking, she pushed her dress off her shoulder and fumbled with her bra strap to tighten it so less of her would show on stage.

The door opened and Evelyn Craig came out, about to light her cigarillo. She saw what Margaret was trying to do and put her cigarillo and matches in her front pocket. "Let me help."

"Thank you," Margaret said.

Evelyn lifted Margaret's right bra strap and gently teased the elastic through the buckle. When she reached for the left strap she stopped, seeing a bruise Jack had pinched into Margaret's skin that morning when he thought she wasn't working hard enough on the music. Evelyn rested her fingers on the bruise for a moment, and Margaret thought she could feel a pulse in Evelyn's fingertips. Evelyn's face was a foot from her own. Margaret suddenly wondered what it would feel like to rest her cheek against Evelyn's. Evelyn's skin was so smooth compared to Jack's. Evelyn finished adjusting the bra strap and gently tugged the neck of Margaret's dress together. "That should be a little better."

"I don't think I can go back in there," Margaret said.

The door opened with a bang and Jack stepped out. "Get in here, Margaret."

Evelyn squeezed Margaret's upper arms. "Sing for me," she said.

When Margaret took the stage for the second set, she sang only for Evelyn Craig. The noise of the bar receded, and she felt calmer, knowing somehow that she would get through it.

Nights at the rehabilitation hospital are hard after Evelyn goes home. Margaret lies in the dark, feeling blood coursing through the vessels in her brain, terrified that they will bleed out again. One night her panic makes her wet herself. She lies in her urine, humiliated. The night aide comes in, a woman Margaret hasn't seen before. The woman sniffs, smelling the urine. "Oh, for Christ's sake." Without looking Margaret in the eyes the aide strips the bed, pulling the sheet up so hard and fast that Margaret rolls out of bed and onto the floor, hitting her knees and left elbow. The woman leaves her on the floor until she gets the new sheets on, then lifts her back into bed. Margaret lies awake the rest of the night, her knees and elbow stinging, praying the woman won't return.

In the morning, Evelyn comes. Her smile fades when she sees Margaret's pleading eyes. "What's wrong?"

Margaret struggles to find the words. Saliva fills the back of her throat and she has trouble swallowing. Evelyn sits on the bed and Margaret's gown shifts, showing her skinned knees. Evelyn's eyes widen. Margaret shows Evelyn her elbow, and Evelyn is out the door, calling for the director of nursing. Margaret listens to Evelyn lambast the woman, her voice filling the hallway: Why didn't they call her, what kind of monsters did they hire, they were idiots. "I'm taking her home," Evelyn says, coming back into Margaret's room.

The director of nursing follows her. "Please reconsider. She needs physical therapy and speech therapy if she's going to make any progress."

"I'll do it myself," Evelyn says. "I may not be perfect but at least I won't batter her. Get us a wheelchair."

It is ten miles to their home on the campus of the McMullen School, where Evelyn is the school librarian and Margaret is the choral director. They ride in silence. It feels odd to be out of the hospital. The cars coming toward them move too fast, seem to come too close. Evelyn reaches over and takes Margaret's hand.

It is past noon when they reach their house. Evelyn drives up close to the front and has Margaret wait while she drags an old door around from the side yard to make a ramp so Margaret won't have to maneuver the two porch stairs with her walker. She helps Margaret out of the car and up the ramp. Through the long glass panels on either side of their front door the hardwood floors of their living room gleam in the afternoon light, beautiful. Evelyn opens the door for her and she is home.

After that first night at Duquesne's it was six months before Margaret saw Evelyn again. She looked for her at the club but never saw her. Adelicia Hughes was there one night, and Margaret found her at a break to ask about Evelyn.

"Oh, she doesn't live here, she just visits from time to time. I never know when she'll show up."

Margaret was twenty-three but felt ancient. Every night that Jack made her sing she thought she couldn't possibly go through it again, but it continued. They moved from their apartment to a roach-infested room off Canal Street. Jack spent most of the money they earned on drink and dope, and the more he drank the more he beat her. At first he hit her where it wouldn't show, but as time went on he didn't seem to care where he hurt her. He bent her pinky finger back so far he broke it, telling some fantastic lie to the doctor who splinted it. Standing naked before the mirror Margaret saw bruises of various ages covering her torso, the purple, green, and yellow colors of Mardi Gras, and a bald patch where Jack had ripped out some of her pubic hair. She could not imagine anyone ever touching her with love again.

An evening came when she could barely dress herself to go and perform. She knew Jack would hurt her but she just didn't care anymore. He marched her out of the apartment and toward the club, using her splinted finger like a handle to control her, bending it and forcing her arm behind her back. She was too beaten down even to cry.

They got to the club early so Jack could get soused at the bar before he had to play. Margaret sat at a table in the corner staring at the wall, not even taking her coat off.

"Margaret? Margaret."

Margaret lifted her eyes. Evelyn Craig stood there, wearing a brown pinstriped suit with a carnation in the buttonhole and thick-soled men's shoes. She was a little heavier, a little shorter than Margaret remembered.

Evelyn sat down across from her. "Are you all right?"

The question seemed to come from far away. Margaret thought she should answer it, but then it seemed like a long time since Evelyn had asked it and the moment for an answer passed. The jazz orchestra came in, and the coronet player began to warm up, his high notes sounding too loud in the low room. Margaret pressed her fingers to her ears.

Evelyn reached across the table and touched the splint on Margaret's finger. "What happened?'

Margaret tried to think of the lie Jack had made up about her broken finger, but it wouldn't come. She looked over to where he sat at the bar, listing to the left on the stool. Evelyn followed her gaze. "He did that to you?"

Margaret examined her splinted finger. "Yes."

Jack spun around on the bar stool, almost losing his balance, and tottered over to where Margaret and Evelyn sat. "We're on in fifteen minutes. Go put some makeup on, you look like death."

"I'll go with her," Evelyn said. She helped Margaret up and walked with her toward the ladies' lounge in the back of the bar, but at the last minute steered her through the bar's rear door and out into the alley. It was almost dark, the sky a deep purplish-blue. "My car's a block away," Evelyn said. "Come with me now. You don't ever have to see that man again." As she spoke Jack burst through the door. Margaret cringed and Evelyn placed herself between them.

"Did you forget where the ladies' is? I told you to get ready," Jack said.

"I've invited Margaret to come with me," Evelyn said.

Jack stood up as straight as his drunkenness would allow. "Look, sister. I don't know who you are, but my wife isn't going anywhere with you." He started toward them.

Evelyn stooped down and grabbed a jagged half of a red brick from the litter scattered in the alley, using its rough broken side for purchase. "Come one more step and I'll split your skull," she said.

Jack looked at her in disbelief. "You crazy bitch. Get out of my way." He lurched forward. Evelyn's left foot shot out and kicked him in the kneecap. He sprawled on the ground with his arms out in front. Evelyn crouched next to him, raised the brick above her head and brought it down, not on his skull but on his long, pampered pianist's fingers, splitting them open. Jack screamed and curled up, clutching his hand.

Evelyn backed away, still holding the brick, and took Margaret's arm. She led Margaret out of the alley, past young people congregating on street corners and policemen looking the other way. Jack's screams rent the air but no one paid attention.

They drove north out of New Orleans, the brick resting between them on the black leather seat of Evelyn's car. A gibbous moon hung over them, painting tiny brush strokes of plant shadow into the road. The air that blew in at the window was chilly, but Margaret welcomed it. She raised her voice over the loud putter of the car motor and began to sing, checking now and then for the smile that played at the corner of Evelyn's mouth, letting her know Evelyn wanted her to continue.

Evelyn displayed the brick on the window sill above her desk, with a tiny flowered china vase that was her mother's, a fan her grandfather brought back from Japan, a shallow dish she and Margaret found in a shop on Crete, with orange and black figures of women carrying water. The brick was crude and ugly among the other precious things but beautiful to Margaret and Evelyn. They never spoke of it.

Margaret sits on the daybed in Evelyn's study, looking out on the backyard. Children play near Evelyn's garden, one girl and a gang of boys. Margaret knows them, has taught them all, but the names won't come.

"Let's play superheroes," the biggest boy says.

"I'm Superman!"

"I call Batman."

"You got to be Batman last time!"

"Who are you going to be, Lorna?"

That was the girl's name. Lorna. The headmaster's daughter.

"I'll be Bullet Proof," she says.

"Yeah, but who are you going to *be*?" the big boy says.

"Bullet Proof," she says again.

The young boy with red hair, his name right on the tip of Margaret's mind, tries to help. "Bullet Proof isn't a person, Lorna."

"Oh."

"Just be Cat Woman," the big boy says. Frank. Frankie Domiano. Margaret taught him in choir. Undisciplined but a nice soprano voice before it started to change.

The study is just off the kitchen and the daybed where she sits is not far from the back door. There is candy in a cut-glass jar near the door, little hard sour balls wrapped in plastic. Evelyn likes the cherry ones. She sucks them until they are small rubies glistening on her tongue. Margaret gauges the distance, pulls her walker over with her strong left arm, looks down at her clumsy right leg. She can feel the leg in a way, not on its surface but inside it, enough to put weight on it without it buckling if she is careful. She can get to the door, but how will she lift the candy? She has to keep her good hand on the walker. She pulls herself up and leans on the walker, first moving her good leg a step, then tilting her hips to lift her right foot off the floor. It is twelve steps to the door. The effort makes her heart speed up. When she gets there she leans over, forearms on the walker's horizontal bar, and twists the doorknob with her good hand, then moves back to let the door swing inward on its own. She bangs on the screen door to get the children's attention. The boys back away. She knows how frightening she must look, with her drooping face, the chin whiskers she no longer has the dexterity to tweeze, the guttural sounds that sometimes come from her mouth. But they know her, she isn't a stranger to them.

"Girl," she calls to Lorna, and Lorna walks forward, up the steps.

"Hi, Miss Margaret."

Margaret beckons with her left hand and Lorna comes closer,

looking back once over her shoulder at her friends. Lorna opens the screen door and Margaret points to the candy dish. "Candy. You." She nods to make the offer clear and gestures toward the boys. Lorna takes enough pieces for everyone. "Thank you, ma'am." She goes back down into the yard and distributes the candy, saying something to the boys. They call up to Margaret in reedy unison, "Thank you, Miss Margaret." Margaret smiles at them through the screen.

The children turn and go back to their play. As Margaret watches, the big boy, Frankie, throws his piece of unwrapped candy into Evelyn's garden as if it is contaminated, as if Margaret's affliction will infect him if he eats it. Hurt swells in her throat but she swallows it down, telling herself she understands.

Behind her, Evelyn comes in the front door, wiping her feet on the mat. Evelyn walks into the kitchen. "Look at you!" she says, proud of Margaret for walking so far on her own. Margaret manages what she knows is a twisted smile. Her right leg is shaking from standing too long. She makes her way to the kitchen table and sits down while Evelyn fixes lunch, canned tomato soup and grilled cheese sandwiches. Margaret was the cook. Since her stroke their meals have become more basic. Evelyn does her best.

"Anything happen while I was gone?" Evelyn asks.

Margaret thinks of the children but shakes her head.

Evelyn puts the food on the table and starts to sit, then looks at Margaret's face and narrows her eyes. She goes into the bathroom and comes back with tweezers, takes Margaret's chin in her hand and tweezes the long whiskers that have been bothering her.

Margaret starts to chuckle, the sound gurgling up from her throat, guttural and wild.

Evelyn smiles. "What's so funny?"

Margaret touches her own chin and then points to Evelyn. "Hero," she says.

Evelyn does Margaret's speech therapy every day after breakfast. It is helping. Margaret can tell by people's faces if the right word doesn't emerge when she tries to speak, and it happens less often now. Words come more easily, not many words, but enough to get her point across. Evelyn has taken her to the market and to a school picnic, and when people have approached she has been able to say "hello" and "yes" and "fine." Her right arm is growing stronger too. She can cup her hand around objects now, even lift them if they aren't too small or heavy.

It is a beautiful April morning. Students have left campus for the Easter break. Evelyn has opened all the windows in the house, using pieces of wood to prop the ones that want to slide closed. Birds sing as they grub in Evelyn's garden. Margaret knows Evelyn would like to be outside grubbing in the dirt herself. They sit at the kitchen table and Evelyn makes Margaret repeat after her.

"Cat," Evelyn says.

"Cat." Margaret has to lift her sluggish tongue for the *T*.

"Cat."

"Cat."

"That's better. Off."

"Off."

"Good. Bother."

"Bother." It comes out sounding like "Bovah." Margaret tries again. "Bothah."

"Watch my mouth," Evelyn says.

Margaret watches. Evelyn says the word, pulling her lips back so Margaret can see what her tongue and teeth have to do to make the *R*. As weathered as the rest of Evelyn's face is, her lips are smooth and a lovely dark pink. Margaret thinks of how they taste, like warm metal, sometimes a hint of basil or nasturtium if Evelyn has been sampling from her garden.

"Pay attention," Evelyn says.

"Bother," Margaret says.

"Knock," Evelyn says.

"Knock."

"Knock, knock." Evelyn's brown eyes twinkle.

Margaret goes along. "Who there?"

"Sam and Janet," Evelyn says.

It is too many syllables. "Who?" Margaret says.

"Say, 'Sam and Janet who.' Take your time," Evelyn says.

Margaret concentrates on one word at a time. "Sam. And. Jan."

"Janet."

"Sam. And. Jan. Janet. Who."

Evelyn spreads her arms and bursts into song. "Sam and Janet evening, you will meet a stranger!" Evelyn has a terrible voice. The two of them always laugh about how she can't carry a tune in a bucket. Margaret, the voice teacher, raises a finger to show Evelyn how it should be done. She breathes from her diaphragm and opens up her throat to sing. And nothing comes out. She swallows once, twice, and tries again. Nothing. The melody arrives at her throat but her vocal cords have forgotten how to let it through. Margaret hadn't realized. She knew her words were lost but she never thought the music itself was gone. She touches the base of her throat and looks up. Evelyn is staring at her, her face stricken.

A loud knock on the front screen door interrupts them. A man's voice calls, "Anybody home?"

"It's open," Evelyn calls back.

The headmaster, Richard Pierce, lets himself in. Margaret and Evelyn have been at the school through four headmasters. Richard is neither the best nor the worst, a competent administrator but far too serious. Even during school vacation he is wearing a tie. He greets Margaret first, tactfully reaching for her good hand. His own hand is moist and softer than a man's should be. "Margaret, you're looking well. How are you feeling?" He speaks loudly. People do that, she's noticed, as if she has lost her hearing as well as her voice.

She smiles at him. "Fine. Yes."

"Would you like a seat?" Evelyn offers. "We have some coffee left."

"No, I just wanted to say hello to Margaret. And to talk to you about something, Evelyn." He tilts his head toward the living room. "Would you mind?"

Evelyn glances at Margaret. Margaret smiles to let her know it's all right. Evelyn rises and follows the headmaster out of the kitchen.

Margaret tries to be polite and listen to the bird sounds outside, but she can clearly hear the headmaster's low voice. "You know I hate to do it, Evelyn, but we need a music teacher. The regional choral competition is coming up. I'm going to have to hire someone." Margaret can't hear Evelyn's response.

Margaret isn't angry. She understands that he has to replace her. Her salary has never been large. They can make it on Evelyn's alone, and with Evelyn's job as school librarian they will still have their faculty housing. It will be all right. She hears the headmaster leave and Evelyn comes back into the kitchen. She sits down across from Margaret, not meeting her eyes.

Margaret reaches over and taps Evelyn's hand. "Cat," she says gently, to let Evelyn know she's ready to resume speech therapy.

A sob like a deep bark rips from Evelyn's throat. She raises the back of her hand to her mouth and presses, but more sobs burst through. Evelyn, who never cries. Margaret reaches over and pulls Evelyn's hand away from her mouth so she can weep openly. Evelyn's nose turns red and tears course along the wrinkles that run from the outside corners of her eyes to the corners of her mouth. The birds stop singing outside, frightened by the noise.

Tears sting Margaret's own eyes. She thinks Evelyn is crying about the job, and squeezes her hand. "I don't mind," she says. It comes out "Iohmy," but Evelyn understands her.

"It isn't that." Evelyn swipes her sleeve across her face to wipe away tears, then touches Margaret's throat. "I just want to hear you sing."

Later that morning, after the slow one-handed job of cleaning herself, Margaret walks with her walker from the bathroom to the study. The smell of crab apple blossoms wafts in through the big window above Evelyn's desk. Margaret makes her way to the window to look out. Evelyn is down below, tending her garden, getting ready to plant. Her back is to Margaret and Margaret thinks she sees sadness in the rounding of Evelyn's shoulders as she crouches, the way the skin folds on the back of her neck. A breeze ruffles papers on Evelyn's desk. With her eyes still on Evelyn, Margaret reaches out with her right hand, the useless one, and runs it along the windowsill above Evelyn's desk. Her clumsy fingers close over an object and she looks at what she is holding. When it is in that hand her mind won't tell her what it is, even though she knows its color and can say to herself that it is rough. She transfers the object from her right hand to her left and her mind opens up. The piece of brick is solid in her hand. She lifts it to her face and smells the sticky cement floor of Duquesne's bar and the mud of Lake Pontchartrain as she and Evelyn pass it heading north. She feels the warmth of Evelyn's body in the driver's seat next to her.

She moves around the side of the desk to get closer to the window and opens her mouth, her whispered hum a test. Words won't come but she pushes breath past her vocal cords and the melody flows outward, the sound pure and clear in the moist air. Below, Evelyn stops digging. She stands and turns to look up at Margaret, her trowel dangling from her hand. Margaret smiles down at her. As she sings she hears the words in her head.

> In the twilight of my years, *cher,*
> My dim eyes will see you clearly,
> My deaf ears will hear your sweet voice.
> Now while we are still young,
> Turn for me, turn for me on the floor,
> *Dansons, dansons, dansons.*

Wish I May

School bus brakes hissed, and Edwina Pickens looked up from her book, the peaceful part of her morning over. From her seat at the front of the bus she looked out at the raggedy line of housing-project kids waiting to climb on. Derrick Mims laughed with Ancell McLean, who had failed two grades and was as tall as a grown-up. Crystal Howard, the only blue-eyed Black person Edwina had ever seen, put on lipstick. Behind her a white girl, Tammy Holderfield, crushed out a cigarette with the sole of her dirty flip-flop. Seventh grade and already smoking. Edwina's parents would shoot her dead if they caught her with a cigarette.

The bus driver opened the door. The bus shook as the project kids got on, shoving each other, jostling people's seats, parading to the back of the bus. Edwina's daddy said that the days of Black people sitting in the back of the bus were over and he better not catch her sitting anywhere but up front, but Derrick and those others liked to sit in the back so they could cut up without the bus driver seeing. Rough. Those kids were just rough. Edwina turned in her seat to steal a look at Derrick. His T-shirt was stark white against his skin. A raised vein ran the length of his arm, like the seam of clothing turned inside out. He saw her looking and grinned. Edwina turned back around.

The project kids started banging on the backs of their seats and singing.

Your ma
Your pa
Your greasy granny
Your skanky mammy
Your scooby dooby
I'll bust your booty

I'll squeeze your cherry
In the dictionary!

Edwina didn't like that nasty sex talk. She opened her book and tried to read, but it was too loud. She wished she were in the cafeteria at the McMullen School, where she studied most afternoons while her mama finished up her work as cafeteria manager. It was peaceful there, the only noises the giant refrigerator's hum and the soft step of her mama's rubber shoes.

In the back of the bus, Ancell, Tammy, and Crystal started up again with their dirty songs, stomping their feet and clapping their hands like cheerleaders.

High school students were allowed to drive school buses in Habersham County. The skinny white girl who drove Edwina's bus, Deirdre, looked up into her rearview mirror. "Pipe down back there!" she yelled.

"Fuck you!" Tammy yelled back.

Edwina closed her eyes and leaned her cheek against the cool glass of the bus window, willing the bus driver to hurry up and get them to school.

At supper that evening, the grown-ups were talking about the Cordelia Six, five Black men and a white woman arrested for firebombing a theater after it wouldn't let some Black teenagers in. One of the men, Alvie Davis, was a preacher out of Atlanta who had marched with Dr. King. He had come up to lead a peaceful protest about the theater and got arrested when the firebombing happened. The trial had ended and the jury, all white, was closed up in a hotel room in Clarksville, deciding what to do.

"It's liable to be bad either way. Somebody's going to be unhappy no matter what," Edwina's daddy said. He was a guard at the federal prison in Clayton and knew what he was talking about.

"Guilty or not, that Alvie Davis is one fine-looking man," Edwina's aunt Brenda said. "He can come light my fire any day." Brenda was all pointy angles, elbows and ashy knees. Her long arm bones swept over the table, threatening to knock things over.

"Don't go glorifying that fool," Edwina's daddy said. "He's made it worse for all of us, running his mouth."

Brenda was letting her hair go natural. It swayed when she shook her head. "Sometimes I feel like firebombing something my own self."

"That's crazy talk and you know it." Edwina's mama reached for a bowl of potatoes. "That's no way to get ahead. Maybe some places, but not here."

"Those theater people could have avoided all this if they'd just let folks in like the law says, instead of pretending they never heard of integration," Brenda said.

"You got that part right," Edwina's daddy said.

Edwina had been in elementary school when integration came. She would never say it to her parents, but sometimes she wished things were like they'd been before, when she walked to school with children she'd known her whole life, and the teachers were kind and comfortable and smelled like good things baking.

"What's the Cordelia Six?" her little sister Arabella said. Nobody paid her any mind.

"*I'm* almost six," Arabella said.

Edwina was late getting to the bus the next afternoon because she'd stayed to help a teacher collect papers. By the time she got on, the front of the bus was full, and she had to take a seat toward the rear, just two up from where the project kids held court. They were smoking and shooting spit balls at people with lunchroom straws. Edwina felt a spit ball glance off her cheek.

"Hey!" Derrick said to the boy who had shot Edwina. "Watch who you aiming at." He left his seat and came up to sit beside Edwina, a lit cigarette cupped in his hand. He held it down low so the bus driver couldn't see. Tendrils of smoke circled toward Edwina's face. When Derrick spoke she could smell cigarette on his breath.

"What's your name again?" he said.

"Edwina," she said.

He lowered his voice so his friends couldn't hear, a little smile hanging on his lips. "Who you go with?"

"Nobody," she said, moving away, but her heart sped up.

They had reached the project. The small apartment complex was Clarksville's first attempt at public housing. The one-story brick buildings were less than two years old but already shabby. Plastic toys cluttered the yards and red dirt stained the walls to waist high. Derrick jumped up, the first to get off when Deirdre opened the door. The other project kids took their time.

"There's your mama waiting for you, Tammy," Ancell said. A large woman in a sleeveless tent dress and bedroom slippers sat on the stoop of the closest apartment, snapping beans. Varicose veins lined her glaringly white legs, and her wiry gray hair was up in curlers. The yard in front of her was a solid mass of baked clay.

"Ooh, Tammy, got a song for you," Crystal said, and she and Ancell started singing.

Ain't your mama purty
She got meatballs up her titties
She got scrambled eggs
between her legs
Ain't your mama purty!

"Y'all shut up," Tammy said, but she laughed. They got off the bus and Tammy scuffed home, stopping to say something to her mother before opening the torn screen door of their apartment and going inside.

As the bus pulled away, Derrick ran toward it. He jumped up like he was doing a basketball layup and slapped the glass of Edwina's window, then ran off after Ancell and the others.

"Y'all people crazy," Edwina muttered, but when she got off the bus at the McMullen School she caught herself singing *Ain't your mama purty* under her breath.

Her mama met her at the cafeteria door to give her a hug. She pulled a spit ball out of Edwina's hair and then sniffed. "Edwina Pickens, is that cigarette smoke I smell?"

"Some of the kids smoke on the bus," Edwina said.

"The driver allows that?"

"They do it in the back where she can't see," Edwina said, though she was pretty sure Deirdre knew about the smoking and just didn't care.

Her mama looked at her. "I don't like that. I really don't."

"It's fine, Mama. Don't worry."

Edwina did her homework, then walked up the school's winding road as far as it would go, to the athletic field. She stood at the top of the concrete bleachers and looked out on the empty playing field. Beyond the tree line to her right, low mountains folded into each other, each one a slightly different shade of blue-gray so that she had to squint to make out the line that separated one from another. To her left the gorge walls peeked through the trees. Her teacher said the horizontal striations in the rock came from millions of years of layering. Edwina wanted to be a teacher, to know things and explain them. She wanted to teach in a place like the McMullen School, where children walked in neat, orderly lines and the classroom buildings were cool from being built into the rock. Her school wasn't cool. This time of year sweating students fought to keep their eyes open, while fans whirred and insects throbbed outside, the sound rising and then tapering off. Hot, hot, hot.

She walked back to the cafeteria, feeling the mountains sure and quiet behind her.

The next afternoon when the bus stopped at the project, the kids who lived there put their cigarettes out, and all but Tammy swaggered off the bus.

"Hold up," Tammy called. "My damn flip-flop broke." Edwina looked back. Tammy was crouched in the aisle, trying to work the plug of her flip-flop back into its hole. Tammy had highlighted her dirty-blonde hair with lemon juice or something. Odd orange streaks radiated out from her part. Under her thin T-shirt, fat humped around her bra.

"Get a move on!" Deirdre yelled from the driver's seat.

Tammy got her shoe fixed and stood up but didn't head for the front of the bus. "What's your problem?" she said to Deirdre. "You on the rag?"

"Just get your fat ass off the bus," Deirdre said.

At the bottom of the bus steps, Derrick, Ancell, and Crystal waited for Tammy. "You gonna take that, Tammy?" Derrick said. He bounded back onto the bus and sat down in front of Edwina to watch the show. He rested his long arm along the back of his seat. Edwina could have lifted her hand to touch it.

Eyes fixed on Deirdre, Tammy took one baby step forward, then another, going as slow as possible. Just as Tammy got to Edwina's seat, Deirdre swung around and put her foot on the gas, making the bus lurch forward. Tammy lost her balance and fell into Edwina, knocking Edwina's shoulder against the window. Tammy flailed in the seat, her legs splayed.

"Ooh, you done it now," Derrick said.

Deirdre stopped the bus again and stood up facing Tammy. "Now get off."

Tammy struggled up and got in Deirdre's face. "You whore."

Deirdre crossed her arms. "Your mama's a whore."

Tammy slapped her, knocking Deirdre back into the driver's seat. Deirdre landed with her sunglasses skewed on her face.

Tammy got off the bus. Her mother was in the yard of their apartment. Tammy yelled to her, "This bitch called you a whore." Tammy's mother started toward the bus.

Derrick met Edwina's eyes. "You too smart for all this," he said. He sprang up and clambered off the bus after Tammy.

Tammy's mother had almost reached them. Deirdre slammed the bus door shut and tore away from the curb. On the sidewalk in front of the project, Tammy stood beside her mother, pointing at the bus. The other project kids split up to walk to their own apartments. As Edwina watched, Derrick put his arm around Crystal Howard.

The kids who remained on the bus were dead quiet. Edwina

kneaded her bruised shoulder. She was glad when the bus finally chugged up the approach road to the McMullen School, where stone buildings and walls rose like a mighty fortress, keeping any ugly stuff out.

She dropped her books off in the cafeteria and called to her mama that she didn't have any homework, then went outside, to the low stone wall that ran along the back of the nearest class-room building. She lay down on the wall, cool stone chilling her through her dress. When she was little she could lie on this wall with room to spare. Now her elbows and ankles slipped off if she didn't hold herself in.

A steep wooded incline rose behind the wall, close enough that Edwina could reach out a finger and touch ticklish ferns, making them close. Near the top, small boulders jutted out like turtle heads, their surfaces covered with aqua-colored blooms of lichen. Holly and rhododendron leaned over her. The roots of the rhododendron formed tunnels, hideouts, meeting rooms. Edwina used to play in there, with the headmaster's little girl and the other faculty kids, but she was getting too tall to fit comfortably, and starting to care, like her mama did, about the dirt that wound up on her clothes.

"When I was a child I thought like a child, but now I have put away childish things," her Sunday School teacher liked to say. *But what do I get to replace those things?* Edwina thought, watching a caterpillar inch across sparkling gray and orange stone. *Don't I get something?*

Somebody tattled, and that night the principal called all the parents and told them what had happened on the bus. Edwina heard her parents talking in their bedroom.

"We've got to figure something out," her daddy said. "She's a smart girl. She deserves to go to school where it's safe and we don't have to worry about this bullshit."

"We can ask the headmaster to let her go to the McMullen School," her mama said. "He let Elena Domiano's boys go."

"Elena Domiano is white," her daddy said.

"I'm about past caring. We've got to do something," her

mama said. "Do you have a better idea?"

Edwina's daddy didn't answer. Edwina lay in her bed, barely daring to breathe.

The next morning, her daddy took leave time from work and drove her to school.

"If I could drive you every day, I would," he said. "Since I can't, you the one got to remember who you are. You're a Pickens. You don't act like those other kids, you hear me?"

"Yes, sir," she said.

Her daddy's right hand gestured as he drove, punctuating a silent conversation he was having with somebody in his head. His hand did like that when he was angry or aggravated. Edwina wondered what he was saying. One time she even asked him, but he said he was just stretching his wrist.

"Daddy, I heard you and mama talking about me maybe going to the McMullen School," she ventured.

"We were just talking. Don't go getting your hopes up." He didn't look at her.

"The Domiano boys go, and their mother is just a regular cafeteria worker, not the manager like Mama. And Frankie Domiano is nothing but trouble."

"The Domianos getting to go isn't why you don't get to go. It's not about what somebody else has. Lord knows that woman needs a place to put those boys, where she can keep an eye on them."

"I'm just saying," Edwina said.

"Well, don't be saying," her daddy said. "Her husband up and left her with those boys. She needs all the help she can get."

Edwina crossed her arms over her chest. She was a better student than the Domianos would ever be.

Her daddy looked over at her. "I haven't said no," he said. "Just let me and your mama think on it."

Edwina had a piano lesson that afternoon and walked home from there. When she got to her house her mama was on the porch waiting for her, a deep line between her brows. "They convicted the Cordelia Six, even Reverend Davis and that white woman," she said. They went inside. Edwina's aunt Brenda, who worked as a housekeeper at the McMullen School, was in the kitchen, eating a yeast roll left over from the cafeteria.

"There's a meeting at the Unitarian Church in Clarksville this evening," Edwina's mama told Edwina. "Your daddy and me are going. The headmaster and some of the other faculty are too. Brenda, I told them you'd babysit."

"What!" Brenda's mouth was still full of roll. "White people going to a meeting about this and I'm supposed to stay and take care of their children?"

"You need the money," Edwina's mama said. "And you don't need to be out and about tonight. There's going to be trouble."

Her parents left for the meeting in town, taking Arabella with them. Edwina went with Brenda to babysit the headmaster's daughter, Lorna, and her little friend Chase, the son of the chemistry teacher. Brenda fixed them all grilled cheese sandwiches for supper, grumbling under her breath the whole time and banging pans louder than she had to. She turned the radio on so she could catch any news of what was going on in Cordelia. As they were clearing the table, an announcer came on, talking about the verdict and describing a race riot downtown.

"That's it," Brenda said, taking her apron off. "I'm going down there."

"What?" Edwina said.

"I'm going down there. I want to see it for myself."

"You're babysitting," Edwina said.

"We all going," Brenda said. "Come on."

"Where are we going?" Chase said.

"Cordelia," Brenda said.

"You're crazy," Edwina said.

"No, I'm not, I'm mad. Come on." Brenda grabbed her beat-up old pocketbook from the kitchen counter and herded

Lorna and Chase out of the kitchen. She moved like Olive Oyl in the *Popeye* cartoons.

"Oh, Lord," Edwina said, following behind.

They got into Brenda's long, boxy Oldsmobile, with the rust spots on the hood. Edwina sat in back with Lorna and Chase. Brenda kept a bear skin rug in the back window. Its fur was still warm from the day's sun. Brenda backed out of the headmaster's driveway, her hair bouncing with every bump in the road.

Edwina entertained Lorna and Chase while Brenda drove the winding highway south. They played "I Spy" and Edwina braided Lorna's long, straight hair. It was dark by the time they approached Cordelia. Brenda slowed down, creeping through vacant streets toward downtown. Edwina began to smell smoke through the open car windows. They rounded a curve and Brenda slammed on the brakes, almost throwing Chase to the floor.

Cordelia's usually drab downtown was alight. Orange fire engulfed two separate one-story buildings. Silhouetted figures ran in front of the flames. The plate-glass window of a car dealership to their right reflected the swirling blue lights of police cars parked in front of it. Traffic lights turned from green to yellow to red with no one noticing. Sirens wailed, coming closer.

Two men ran past their car, headed toward the fires. One of them was bleeding, the line of blood darker than the skin of his arm. Brenda turned around in the driver's seat. "Chase and Lorna, get under that rug."

"What for?" Chase said.

Edwina pulled the bear skin rug from the back window and spread it over the children. "Just do it. Pretend you're a bear."

Chase's voice was muffled. "This rug doesn't smell like a bear."

His head was a knob under the rug. Edwina pushed down on it. "How do you know what a bear smells like? You ever sniffed a bear?"

"Ow, Chase, get your elbow out of my eye," Lorna said.

"Y'all be still under there," Brenda said.

Under the rug, Chase and Lorna giggled and growled like bears.

A group of young men loped around a corner of the car dealership, bricks and sticks in their hands. The man in the lead looked back over his shoulder and yelled something to the others. He ran toward the car dealership's plate-glass window, his body arching like a dancer's as he threw the brick. The brick sailed through the window, shattering it.

All around, in the dipping and weaving of bodies, Edwina felt something let loose. In front of her the fires had reached the buildings' roofs. Flames towered, leaning sideways with the wind. Edwina buried her fingers in the coarse fur of the bear skin rug. There was beauty in the burning. Sparks from the flames showered out onto pavement like fireworks at the fair. She narrowed her eyes, trying to isolate one spark, the way she sometimes did on a summer night that was already full of stars, focusing on just one so she could play "star light, star bright, first star I see tonight." She followed a spark, up into the night sky and then down again, as it tripped along the sidewalk and went out. *I wish*, Edwina thought. *Oh, I wish.*

Up front in the driver's seat Brenda shook her head back and forth. "That's something."

There was a "crack" as a rock hit the windshield of Brenda's car, pitting the glass. "Don't you be throwing things at me, fool!" Brenda hollered at the night. She put the car in reverse and backed up without looking, sending a man behind them diving to the side.

"I don't like this," Lorna quavered from under the bear skin rug.

"Me either," Chase said. "I'm scared."

Brenda got the car headed the right way and peeled out. Edwina let Chase and Lorna out from under the rug and draped it around their shoulders. Lorna's face was pale, and Chase looked like he was going to cry. Edwina tousled their hair. "Y'all all right," she said. In the rearview mirror she could see the fires, two orange giants gesturing at each other.

In the yard of the headmaster's house, Edwina's parents waited with Arabella, their faces shining in the light from the porch.

Brenda and the children got out of the car. Edwina's mama pointed to the damaged windshield of Brenda's car. When she spoke her voice was tight and controlled. "Tell me you have not been where I think you've been."

Brenda tossed her head. "I wanted to see it for myself."

"What were you thinking?" Edwina's daddy roared. "Driving white children down there in that mess. Are you out of your mind? We're thinking about asking the headmaster to let Edwina come to the McMullen School. You think he's going to let her in when he finds out you carried his child to a race riot?" He raised one of his big hands. Brenda flinched. He clenched his fist and turned away from her.

"We're going to get these children settled in and take Edwina and Arabella home," Edwina's mama said to Brenda. "When their parents get back, you're going to explain to them exactly what you did. I just hope the headmaster doesn't fire you and me both."

Edwina's mama and daddy led Chase and Lorna into the headmaster's house. Brenda stood in the yard. The porch light illuminated the smattering of dark acne on her cheek, the sad tug-down of her mouth. Brenda wasn't much older than Edwina herself was. Edwina reached out and touched Brenda's shoulder.

Brenda turned toward her and gave a tired smile. "I guess I better go in and take my medicine. I'm sorry I dragged you into this."

"It's okay," Edwina said.

Brenda went into the house and closed the door, leaving Edwina and Arabella standing in the yard.

"You in *trouble*," Arabella sing-songed.

"Not me," Edwina said.

Edwina brushed her teeth and slipped into the room she shared with Arabella. The room was dark except for a wedge of light from the hall. Arabella was asleep. Edwina got into bed but she couldn't settle down. She reached back and fluffed her pillow. Her hair smelled of smoke from the downtown fires.

Her mama tiptoed in and bent down to kiss her good night.

"Mama?" Edwina said.

"Yes?"

"I know Brenda did wrong, but you should have seen it."

Her mama ran a finger along the curve of Edwina's eyebrow. "I know," she said. She straightened up and went out, leaving the door partly open behind her.

Edwina got up. She walked down the hall to the living room, where her parents were sitting on the sofa, talking in low voices. She stood in the doorway until her daddy looked up and noticed her. "What are you doing out of bed?" he said.

"Will you ask him?" Edwina said.

Her parents looked at each other.

"Will you ask the headmaster to let me come to school? Please?"

Her mama pressed her lips together. Her daddy knotted his fist and knocked it against his chin a few times like he was thinking, then opened his hand and reached out to Edwina. Edwina moved close enough for him to put his arm around her waist.

"I'll ask him," he said.

Back in bed, Edwina snuggled under the covers, pulling them up to her chin. Across the room Arabella's breathing was husky, not quite a snore. A car passed by outside, its headlights sweeping up the wall and across the ceiling. Edwina closed her eyes, imagining silhouette puppets dancing in front of a burning building, their anger sometimes lifting them off the ground as they threw things into the flames.

Breaking Bread

Lorna and Chase played tetherball on the playground after school, their Blue Horse notebooks abandoned in the red dirt a few feet away. Lorna beat Chase every time because he was short. She had worked out a scientific rhythm, smacking the orange ball at just the right moment every time it came around, watching its white nylon rope wind hard and fast around the pole, too high for Chase to reach. It was getting a little dull, winning all the time, and Lorna played with one eye on the steep approach road, wishing the school bus from town would hurry up and drop off Edwina Pickens. If she got all her homework done, Mrs. Pickens let her play with Lorna and Chase.

Lorna won again.

"Aw, man." Chase's cheeks were pink underneath his freckles and sweat spiked his red hair.

Lorna sniffed the rubbery smell the ball had left on her hands. The day was so hot that not even the cool wall of rock that rose behind the campus could offer any relief. Over the buzz of insects and the calling of birds, Lorna heard Edwina's school bus chugging up the hill. It stopped and let Edwina off. Edwina was thirteen, tall and graceful. Her friends hung out the windows of the bus calling goodbye, their arms flapping like the puny wings of a big orange bird. The arms were mostly white, with a few darker ones. There weren't very many Black people in this part of Georgia.

The bus pulled away and Chase yelled, "Edwina!"

Edwina dropped her schoolbooks on the ground by the tetherball pole. "Don't holler my name so loud. My mama'll hear you and make me go inside and do homework." She took the tetherball in her hands. "Who wants to play?"

"Me," said Lorna. Chase sat down on the grass to rest.

Edwina let Lorna start off, but immediately got the ball going her way. Her long body stretched upward, her hand slamming the ball when it passed, her palm as pale as Lorna's except for dark pigment that ran along her lifeline and the other creases where her fist closed. She beat Lorna in a matter of seconds.

"That was good," Edwina said. "You about had me."

"Edwina, spin me around," Chase said, clambering up from the ground and holding out his arms.

"Oh, Lord," Edwina said, but grasped his wrists and let him grab hers. She swung him around in a wide circle until he was airborne.

"Faster!" Chase yelled.

"You better hope I don't lose hold," Edwina said. She slowed down and laid Chase on the ground.

Lorna held out her arms for a turn.

"I can't do you like that anymore, Lorna. You getting too tall. Your feet'll drag the dirt."

"Pleeease."

"Oh, all right." Edwina took Lorna's wrists and swung her around, leaning back in a half crouch as she turned in a circle. Lorna's legs left the ground. She was flying, her shoulders about to pop out of their sockets, wind whistling in her ears. "Faster!" she screamed, so happy she thought she would explode, but Edwina slowed down, straining to hold Lorna up high enough that she could get her feet down and not burn her knees on the dirt. Edwina lowered her to the ground. Lorna lay on her back, feeling the world spin around her.

Edwina plopped down beside her, rubbing her wrists. "Next time, you swinging me."

Chase's older sister, Mandy, walked up the road to where they were playing. Mandy was a senior. She was pretty. Her halter top showed off her tan. Mandy's boyfriend, Wally, had just left for the army and would be going to Vietnam soon, and Mandy had been moping around a lot, sighing. "Chase, Mom says come home and clean your room," Mandy said.

"In a minute."

Lorna sat up. Edwina helped her brush pieces of grass off her back and out of her hair.

Mandy slipped off one of her red Dr. Scholl's sandals and shook an invisible piece of dirt out of it. "I don't know how y'all can stand to play outside in this heat." Wally's big McMullen School class ring hung loosely on her pointer finger. She kept her finger curled so it wouldn't fall off.

"You ought to put a piece of mohair inside that ring," Edwina said. "That's what my cousin does."

"Maybe I will," Mandy said, putting her shoe back on.

The school maintenance office was in the basement under the cafeteria, down a flight of brick stairs that went below ground at the end of the building. James, one of the maintenance men, came up the stairs and across the playground, eating a Nutty Buddy. James was nice. He gave Lorna and Chase pieces of Fruit Stripe gum when he had it, the kind with the zebra on the pack. His brown hands were covered with knotty white scars from working hard all his life.

"Hot," he said when he reached them.

"You can say that again," Mandy said, fanning herself.

James looked at Chase, whose face had grown bright red with the heat. "You look like you about to have apoplexy. Here," he held his Nutty Buddy out to Chase. "Have you a bite."

Chase took a bite, the crusty chocolate coating breaking off around melting vanilla ice cream. Lorna wished James would offer her some.

The cafeteria's screen door opened, and Edwina's mother called across the yard. "Edwina Pickens, come here and do your schoolwork. James, I need you too, to lift some boxes for me."

"Yes, ma'am," Edwina said. She got her books and she and James walked toward the cafeteria.

When they were out of earshot, Mandy said, "Chase, don't eat after a Black man like that. That's nasty."

"How come?" Chase licked his lips.

Mandy shrugged. "It just is." She walked up the hill toward the boys' dorm.

Lorna looked over to where Mrs. Pickens held the cafeteria door open for James and Edwina. A webbed hairnet rested almost invisible against the neat curve of her hair. Stainless steel pots gleamed behind her.

That night after Lorna took a bath, her mom sat on the bed with her, brushing the knots out of her wet hair, and told her she would be leaving for a while, to go up to Pennsylvania. "Grandma's not doing well. She needs me."

"When will you be back?" Lorna said.

"It depends on how Grandma does. When school's out in a few weeks you can come up too."

"But that's a long time," Lorna said, tears pressing against the backs of her eyes.

Her mom set the brush down and put her hands on Lorna's shoulders. "I'll be here for your birthday. I wouldn't miss that. What would you like to do to celebrate?"

"The Pancake House."

"Good choice. Do you want to invite friends?"

"Can I have Chase and Edwina?"

There was just the slightest pause before her mom answered. "Of course you can."

Later, when Lorna was almost asleep, she heard her parents talking.

"Do you think that's a good idea, with people so stirred up about the Cordelia Six?" her dad said. "I think you're using Edwina for your own agenda."

"That's ridiculous. She's Lorna's friend. Why should we have to think twice about inviting her out to eat? It's 1970, for God's sake," her mom said.

On Lorna's birthday, her mom took ten candles plus one to grow on for Lorna to stick into her stack of pancakes at the Pancake House. Lorna's mom drove her red and white VW bus. Chase insisted on riding in the very back, where luggage was supposed to go. Lorna and Edwina sat on the back seat, giggling at Chase as he slid around like a piece of Samsonite. Edwina was all dressed up, in a yellow dress with frilly layers like a daffodil and matching yellow barrettes in her hair. Her white sandals looked brand new. At a red light, another VW bus pulled up beside them, with two long-haired men in the front seat. The driver honked and gave them the peace sign. Lorna's mom honked back. Lorna's dad turned his face away.

"Look at those hippies," Edwina said. "Somebody needs a haircut."

At the Pancake House, the hostess seated them. Lorna knew exactly what she wanted: the happy face pancakes with whipped cream for hair and a miniature scoop of butter for the nose. Chase was set on the pigs-in-a-blanket. They waited for the waitress to bring their water.

"Those people sat down after we did," Chase said, pointing to a table where the waitress was taking an order. "No fair. I'm hungry."

"I'm sure she'll get to us soon," Lorna's dad said.

"Look, now she's going over to those people," Chase said.

Lorna's mom slid her chair back.

"Sarah," her dad said.

"Excuse me." Lorna's mom stood up and went to the front of the restaurant. She spoke to the manager at the cash register and pointed toward their waitress. Lorna's dad chewed the inside of his cheek. Edwina, who had been talking and laughing a minute before, folded her hands in her lap.

The manager spoke to the waitress. Lorna's mom returned to the table. The waitress came over. "Sorry, folks. I didn't notice you over here. What can I get you?" She didn't meet their eyes.

Lorna and Chase ordered. The waitress looked up from her pad, impatient for Edwina to decide. Edwina sat frozen, the big laminated menu in her hand. Lorna's dad reached over and pointed. "Lorna always gets the happy face pancakes, Edwina, but you're a grown-up young lady. Why don't you try the lemon crepes?"

Edwina nodded her head. She looked a little sick.

The waitress gathered up their menus and left. From a booth across the aisle, a little boy gawked at them. His dad slapped his hand. "Stop staring." Lorna looked around. Edwina was the only Black person in the restaurant. Edwina sat with her eyes down and her shoulders hunched. She looked smaller than she normally did, as if she had shrunk.

When the waitress brought their food, Lorna's mom pushed candles into Lorna's pancakes and lit them. Edwina's lips barely moved when she sang *Happy Birthday*. She stared at her food.

"Do you feel all right, Edwina?" Lorna's mom said gently.

"Yes, ma'am," Edwina said without lifting her eyes.

"We'll get a box for what you don't eat, and you can take it home," Lorna's dad said.

Edwina nodded.

Lorna knew how it felt to lose your appetite like that. Once her parents had taken her to the K&W Cafeteria in Clarksville. Her eyes had been bigger than her stomach and she had loaded up her tray with way more than she could eat, including a huge piece of strawberry pie. At the bread section the serving lady asked if she wanted bread and Lorna reached out and took a long roll, only to have the lady snatch it from her, put it on a plate, and hand it back to her. Lorna's face had burned hot. Her appetite left her that instant and all she could do at dinner was stare at that piece of pie. That's how Edwina looked now.

The air inside the Pancake House was heavy with the smells of grease and syrup, almost hard to breathe. Lorna wanted to reach out and touch the hand of her shrinking friend. Beside her, Chase dug happily into his food.

Lying in bed that night, Lorna heard her parents though the wall, her dad's low murmur and her mom's voice rising until Lorna could catch words. "I have to leave. I cannot stay and do this anymore."

In the morning, her mom was packed for her trip, with one big suitcase and the small round pink one Lorna loved that was just for her makeup. Outside in front of the house her mom knelt down and took Lorna's face in her two hands. Her fingers were cool and soft. They smelled of Avon lotion. She gathered Lorna close, rubbing her back and kissing the top of her head. With her lips pressed hard against the part in Lorna's hair, she whispered, "Always remember how much Mommy loves you."

Shoes scuffed on the walkway and Lorna's dad joined them, standing there awkwardly. Her mom gave Lorna a last squeeze and stood up. She loaded her luggage into the back of the VW bus. The VW's tires seemed too skinny to support its swollen body. Dead bugs dotted its wide front.

"Are you sure that thing will make it to Pennsylvania?" Lorna's dad asked. "Call me if you have any trouble."

"I'll be fine." Her mom got in and knocked the driver's side wing window open with the heel of her palm. She started the VW, its odd engine sounding loud in the still morning air. She backed up into the road and waved before shifting gears. As she drove down the school's approach road, she wiped her arm across her eyes.

A week after Lorna's birthday, late in the afternoon when Lorna's dad was home from school, Mr. and Mrs. Pickens and Edwina drove up to the headmaster's house and got out. Mrs. Pickens still had on her white uniform and Mr. Pickens wore his guard uniform from the federal prison where he worked.

Lorna's dad met the Pickenses at the door and invited them inside. Mr. Pickens shook hands with Lorna's dad, his huge fingers wrapping around the headmaster's smaller hand.

"I hope you don't mind us coming by like this, sir, but we wanted to speak to you about something," Mr. Pickens said.

"You and your wife have been so kind to Edwina, taking her to the Pancake House and all," Mrs. Pickens said.

Lorna's dad looked puzzled, but he was polite. "Come into my study. Lorna, you can get Edwina a snack while we talk."

The adults went into the study and closed the door. Lorna took Edwina to the kitchen. Since Lorna's mom left, her dad didn't seem to care what they ate and had let Lorna put Vienna sausages in the cart when they went to the grocery store. She shook a can of sausages out onto a paper plate and squeezed pools of mustard and catsup next to the sausages.

"What do your parents want?" Lorna said.

"They're asking can I go to school here," Edwina said.

"Really?" Lorna was thrilled. "I wish you could be in my class. You'll be in Frankie Domiano's class."

"Oh, Lord. That boy's crazy."

"You and me can play at recess," Lorna said.

"First your daddy's got to say I can come," Edwina said. They listened for any sound from the headmaster's study but couldn't hear anything.

"Oh, well." Edwina swirled a Vienna sausage in the mustard and catsup, writing her name in cursive, yellow against red. Lorna did the same, her catsupy letters crossing Edwina's and continuing on to the edge of the paper plate.

When the study door finally opened, Lorna and Edwina looked at each other, holding their breath.

"I can't promise anything," Lorna's dad said, his voice low. "But I'll consider taking it to the Board."

"That's all we asking," Mr. Pickens said. "Thank you, sir."

Lorna's mom called from Pennsylvania. She asked Lorna how things were going.

"Edwina's parents asked Dad if she could come to school here," Lorna said.

"What did he say?"

"I don't think he's decided yet."

"Put him on," Lorna's mom said.

Her dad took the phone, turning away from Lorna as he talked. "She's a good test case. Smart, and it's the lower school, not the high school where feelings might run higher. I've felt out some of the Board members, but I just don't know."

Lorna's mom said something.

"It's not that simple, Sarah." He frowned at Lorna, shooing

her out of the room, but she could still hear what he said. "I could lose my job."

That night Lorna lay in bed, missing her mom, the fragrant steam that billowed out of the bathroom when her mom took a shower, even the sound of her parents arguing. The house was too quiet. She imagined her dad lying wide awake in the next room, all alone.

The afternoon of the Board of Trustees meeting, Lorna stood with her dad on the steps in front of the administration building to welcome the ladies from the Atlanta Women's Club. Lorna thought her dad might send her home, but he seemed glad to have her there. Mrs. Delores Vaughan Parke's Lincoln Continental drove up. The driver helped Mrs. Parke out. She did not look happy. She pointed a gnarled finger at Lorna's dad. "If you make this motion, Richard, I will have your head. You can follow that wife of yours to Pennsylvania, because you won't have a job here." Without waiting for a response, she hobbled over to the stairs and began to climb them, pulling herself up by the handrail.

Lorna's dad swallowed, his Adam's apple sliding up and down.

Two younger ladies had arrived behind Mrs. Parke. Their expensive-looking suits were so narrow at the knees Lorna wasn't sure how they could walk. Lorna's mom called southern women like these "butter beans." The two ladies stopped in front of the headmaster and the taller one, her blonde hair up in an elegant twist, said quietly, "Richard, don't let that old battle-ax frighten you. Contrary to what Mrs. Delores Vaughan Parke may believe, she is not the sole voting member of the Board."

"A lot of us younger women are behind you," the shorter woman said. "I mean, it's one little girl, for heaven's sake, and we already let the white cafeteria worker's children attend. We've got to think about how it makes the school look. Times are changing."

"We can at least get it in front of the full membership for you," the first lady said.

Lorna's dad gave a weak smile, but to Lorna it felt like Sleeping Beauty's christening. The bad fairy had given her curse. The only thing the good fairies could do was come along behind and try to make the best of the situation.

When all the women had arrived, they went into their meeting with Lorna's dad and closed the door. Lorna climbed the stairs to use the bathroom on the second floor. Edwina's aunt Brenda and another Black woman were cleaning the bathroom, talking while they worked.

Lorna said *aunt* like *ant*, but Edwina pronounced it the fancy way. Brenda was Mrs. Pickens's younger sister. She had the only Afro Lorna had ever seen on a real person and big hoop earrings. Lorna had heard Mrs. Pickens say Brenda didn't have the sense she was born with.

A sunburned high school girl in torn bell-bottomed jeans was about to leave the bathroom as Lorna entered. She held a white paper bag. Lorna went into a stall.

"Would y'all like a donut?" the girl offered to Brenda and the other woman.

"No, thank you. I just ate," Brenda said.

"Me, too," the other lady said.

The door closed with a squeak as the girl left.

"Listen at her," Brenda said. "Digging a donut out of that bag with her old nasty hands, didn't even wash her hands good after using the toilet. Her old raggedy self, knees sticking out of her pants. No, I don't want a donut."

The other woman murmured her agreement and they left the bathroom with a bang of mops and buckets.

Lorna came out of the stall. She looked at her pale face in the mirror over the sink. She squirted twice as much soap as usual from the soap dispenser and rubbed it all over her hands, waiting for the water to run warm before she rinsed.

She waited on the curb in front of the administration building until the Board meeting let out. Mrs. Parke stomped down the stairs and over to where her driver waited. Other women whispered in twos and threes. When they had all gone, Lorna's dad came out and locked the door behind him. He sat down next to Lorna on the curb, his knees bent up in a letter *M*. The skin under his eyes looked smudgy. He put his hand on the back of Lorna's neck and lifted her hair up so breeze could touch her skin. He had done that one time when she was little enough to carry. She was sick and he paced with her while she hiccoughed, touching a towel of ice to her hot forehead until her mom came to take over.

"What's going to happen?" Lorna said.

"I don't know," he said.

In opening assembly the next Monday morning, Lorna's teacher, Mrs. Dees, was leading the Pledge of Allegiance, her hand pressed against her bosomy chest where her heart was supposed to be, when the doors of the auditorium opened. Lorna's dad walked in, gently pushing Edwina Pickens in front of him. Edwina was dressed in a blue church dress with gold buttons. Her black shoes shone. She looked scared, but not like she had at the Pancake House. She looked happy, too, and wiggled her fingers at Lorna.

"Mrs. Dees, we have a new student," Lorna's dad said. "Most of you know Edwina."

Mrs. Dees' eyes looked frozen open, but she gave Edwina a big smile. Edwina sat down with the seventh and eighth graders. Lorna's dad leaned against the auditorium's double doors with his arms crossed while Mrs. Dees read the morning announcements. Lorna twisted around and waved until she caught his eye. When he looked at her she gave him a thumbs-up. He smiled but motioned for her to turn back around and pay attention. Lorna faced front. A few rows up, Edwina sat with her spine perfectly straight and her chin lifted. Lorna planned what they would do at recess, the corners of the playground that Edwina might not know about yet, where the best sour grass grew, and honeysuckle twined around the fence, enough nectar for a meal.

The Walk

Chase Robbins had the same haircut as his dad, two whitewalls and a flat top. Every month they went together to Joe Beam's Barber Shop and Chase got a Charms Big Pop wrapped in blue cellophane for sitting still in the chair. One time at the Pancake House in Clayton, a man at the next table had long hair tied in a ponytail like a girl. Chase's sister Mandy left two red moons on Chase's arm, pinching him to make him stop staring.

At Joe Beam's this Saturday, the men were all talking about the Great Wallenda, who would walk across the Tonola Gorge on a tightrope that afternoon.

"The whole world's going to come," the mayor said, while Joe Beam clipped the hairs that grew in his ears.

"They better," said the fire chief. "You spent my firefighting budget on them hot dogs to feed them all."

Chase sat with his dad, waiting his turn. "Dad, can I have a hot dog?" he asked.

His dad was reading an old *Field and Stream* and didn't answer.

When Chase and his dad got back from the barber shop, Chase's dog Bingo ran out and met them. Mandy's boyfriend, Wally, had given Chase the dog when he went into the army. Chase kept Bingo with him most of the time so Bingo wouldn't get on his mom's last nerve. Bingo's black fur grew in wavy cowlicks down his back. Wally said ladies paid good money to make their hair do that.

Wally was in Vietnam now. Chase knew about Vietnam from one night when word had reached the school that another boy who had graduated had been killed there. He remembered his mom running over to the dorms, crying. Chase knew about war. His friend Danny, who lived down the road at the Victory Home for men with drinking problems, had been a tail gunner in World War II. Danny had dreams about the war. When he choked with those dreams in the swing on the Victory Home porch, Chase knew to call out his name softly until he woke up. Danny always said thanks.

From the front yard Chase and his dad could hear his mom yelling at Mandy inside the house. Mandy came out on the steps. She had just graduated from the McMullen School. She wore Wally's class ring on her pointer finger, with a little piece of mohair inside so it wouldn't fall off. Mandy hugged Chase sometimes for no reason. When she and Wally got married, they were going to let Chase spend summers with them.

Mandy had on short red shorts and a white halter top.

"Mandy, put on some real clothes," Chase's dad said.

She ignored him. "Mom's freaking out. I wouldn't go in there if I were you." She walked up the hill toward the boys' dorm. One time a fifth-grade boy called Mandy a hippie because her hips swung when she walked, and Chase had to hit him with a rock.

Chase's mom banged open the screen door. Sweat had un-flipped her *That Girl* hairdo. She talked without opening her teeth. "If Mandy doesn't pack her clothes, I'm going to put them out by the curb." She sat down on the steps and lit a cigarette. The headmaster hadn't renewed Chase's dad's teaching contract and their family was having to move to Tennessee in a week to live with Chase's grandma while his dad looked for work. Chase's mom was mad at his dad for getting fired, and mad at all of them for not helping her get things ready.

Chase's dad held his hand out for her to pass him a cigarette.

"Get your own," she said. All the grown-ups Chase knew smoked. Chase suspected his dad didn't really like cigarettes. When he graded papers he held his cigarette up over the table while it burned away, until Chase's mom yelled at him to take a puff already and stop wasting the Luckys.

"The mayor says the whole world's coming to see Wallenda," his dad said.

"Then we better get up there early," his mom said.

As they loaded a picnic lunch into the station wagon, Mandy came down the hill with a high school boy named Brian Tolliver. Chase's dad said Brian could ride with them. Chase wished he could bring a friend, but his friend Lorna, the headmaster's daughter, had gone up to Pennsylvania to be with her mother and Chase wasn't sure when she'd be back.

"Can I take Bingo?" he asked.

"No," his dad said.

They drove up to the power company property for the best view. The Tonola River had scooped out the gorge before the power company dammed it up. Now the river washed slow and green against the gorge walls, like a boxed animal looking for a way out. Fir trees clung to the sides until it got too steep even for them. At the beginning of the summer, Chase had guided a family of tourists down into the gorge, leading them over boulders that were taller than he was. His mom yelled for a day when she found out. "You could have slipped on those rocks and we never would have found you!"

"Bingo would have saved me." Chase could imagine Bingo's soft tongue cleaning his bloody face, Bingo's bark bringing help.

Wallenda's people had installed pylons on either side of the gorge and strung a cable between them. The cable was bigger around than Chase's arm. Chase wondered how they'd got it across the river. It hung down in a stretched-out letter *U*. Even with guy-wires the wind blew it like a jump rope. He could not believe a man was going to walk along it with it moving like that.

There were a lot of people around, but it didn't look like the whole world had come.

"Where is everybody?" Chase's mom asked. They passed a food booth. The mayor was there looking sad. Crates of thawing hot dogs formed a mountain behind him.

"Can I have a hot dog?" Chase asked.

"No. We brought our lunch," his mom said.

It was finally time for Wallenda to walk. From where they

stood, they could see him mount the pylon at the other side of the gorge. He took off a dark cape and gave it to his assistant. He wore a shiny red jumpsuit. It was tight but the wind still whipped the cloth around his ankles. His shoes looked like Mandy's ballet shoes. He raised his hand and cheers from the thin crowd echoed through the gorge. Wallenda took up his balancing pole. He did everything slow. Loud wind rushed up through the gorge. Chase walked closer to the rim to see better.

"Not so close," his dad called.

Wallenda stepped out onto the cable and everybody hushed. His right foot tested the wire. His ankle bent to just the right angle. With the next step, his left foot was surer. Wallenda's face was calm behind his twirly mustache. His muscles worked as he balanced his stick. Chase found himself lifting his toes when Wallenda lifted his. He wished he had a stick to hold. Wallenda moved out away from the pylon, into air.

Off to Chase's right, somebody giggled. He looked over. Tall bushes near the gorge lip rustled and he saw a strip of Mandy's white halter top, the red leather strap of her Dr. Scholl's. Mandy's voice shushed Brian Tolliver's goofy laugh. The megaphone man announced that Wallenda was going to stand on his head for the boys in Vietnam. Chase looked back at the tightrope. Wallenda was on his knees. His hands went down to the wire. He unfolded his knees and elbows, like a giant praying mantis. He straightened his legs. He was standing on his head. Angry wind moved the cable in waves, but Wallenda stood firm. Below, the green river waited. Around Chase the crowd hardly breathed.

"Did you see that!?" Chase yelled.

"Shh!" his mom said.

Chase imagined what the cable felt like, pressing against Wallenda's forehead. When Wallenda finished standing on his head for the soldiers, he folded himself down to the tightrope again and stood right side up. He smiled. Gusts from the gorge whipped tears from Chase's eyes. He wondered what Wally was up to over in Vietnam. Wallenda started the rest of the

way across, leaning against hard wind. He looked tired, the
way Chase's friend Danny looked when he left his seat on the
Victory Home porch swing to walk uphill to the mailbox.

When Wallenda finally reached the pylon on the other side,
he handed his pole to the assistant and held up his hands, waving to people on both sides of the gorge, not leaving anyone
out. Chase held up his own hands, cupping them around the
wind, which blew so fiercely he could relax his arms and the
wind kept holding them straight up.

The morning of moving day, Chase's mom told him, "Don't
you dare run off. We're leaving at two o'clock sharp."

Chase whistled for Bingo.

"Leave him here," his mom said. "I don't want to have to
hunt for him when it's time."

Mandy floated through. She wasn't wearing Wally's class ring.

"Where's Wally's ring?" Chase asked.

"It's packed," she said.

Chase headed to the Victory Home. When he got there, the
men were eating hot dogs from crates the town had dropped
off, left over from Wallenda's walk. They told Chase to help
himself. The hot dogs were individually wrapped in plastic and
swiped with chili that still had ice crystals in it. Chase shoved
one in his mouth and put two more in his pants pockets to
share with Bingo later.

Danny carved a slingshot.

"You'll have to make me some extras," Chase told him sadly.
"We're moving away today."

"Where you moving to, boy?" Danny asked.

"Tennessee."

"I been to Tennessee. It ain't so bad."

"I want to stay here," Chase said.

"It don't matter where you go," Danny said. "You're always
you when you get there."

Another man down the porch called out, "That can be good
or bad."

"For you, Chase, it'll be good," Danny said. He rested his palm on the top of Chase's head and for once his hand didn't shake.

On the way home, Chase ate the hot dogs he had stashed in his pockets. At his house, a moving van blocked the drive and his parents stood in the yard. A pickup truck pulled away from the curb. As it passed him, Chase saw Bingo riding in the back, roped to the truck's toolbox. Wind blew Bingo's fur the wrong way. He was panting and looked confused.

"Hey!" Chase yelled. "Hey! That's my dog!"

He ran after the truck, picking up handfuls of gravel and grass to throw at it. When it sped out of sight, he ran back to his parents. He had a stitch in his side and could hardly talk. "Bingo!"

His parents didn't run after the pickup like he thought they would. Instead they looked at each other.

"We gave him away, Chase," his dad said. "We can't take him to Tennessee."

"It's for the best, honey," his mom said. "He's going to live on a farm where he can run around."

Chase's parents suddenly looked like aliens. Bingo was going to run around on a farm without him. Chase started to cry. His dad took his arm, but he yanked it away. He dodged around his mom and clambered up the hill toward the administration building and the high wall behind it. Slabs of muscle tightened his calves, boosting him upward. He ran behind the big stone building, his sneakers slapping. At the wall, water dripped off the rocks onto his head. Orange and white stones offered him footholds, as if they had been waiting for him. He didn't slip once.

On the wall's cool top, he looked down. If he fell, his freckles would scatter like new pennies all over the patio. He stuck out his arms to make a pole and pointed his toes. Through the worn rubber of his sneakers he could feel the wall's lumps. He imagined wrapping his toes around cable. Below him his parents' yells rose like dog howls. Chase wiped tears and snot off his face and started along the wall. He moved in slow motion like Wallenda. Rhododendron bushes reached down from the mountainside to tickle his face. He ducked under them, slow, slow. He could hear Mandy crying. If he multiplied the sound by googolplex, it became a cheering crowd.

At the center of the wall's curve, Chase stopped. If he stood on his head, the hard rock would hurt. Instead he closed his eyes. He would jump in place, blindfolded, three times. Once for Wally, who would come home from Vietnam and not know where to find them. Once for Bingo, riding puzzled in the back of that pickup truck. Once for the great Chase Robbins, who was having to leave this place to move to Tennessee. Chase centered himself on the wall. He jumped once. He jumped again and teetered a little but steadied himself without peeking. He jumped the third time, and the crowd below went wild. He smiled and opened his eyes, just as his dad flopped on top of the wall. His dad grabbed him, pushed him down, pressed him flat on his stomach against the top of the wall. "Be still!" His dad was crying, reaching for breath. He lay on top of Chase and Chase could feel his heart banging through both their shirts.

Chase wiggled his hands free on both sides. His dad's weight was a velvet cape across his shoulders. He swiveled his wrists, waving to the crowd in all directions.

Breath

The mountain spreads under them all, watching, listening, breathing.

Two men sit on a porch, talking of an era when they flew, when their feet touched clouds and they danced a dodging dance among corkscrewed shavings of metal. The thinner man smokes. The memories that twine cancerously through his mind have not strangled him. His heart beats as strong as it did in his youth, vibrating through the broad boards of the porch, into the earth and stone beneath. When this one is ready to go, the mountain will open up and take him.

At an overlook an old woman climbs out of a long black car. The mountain knows her. When she was a child she clambered over its rocks with her sister. Now she limps, one leg impeding her, to the edge. There is a sadness in her. The driver and granddaughter who emerge from the car would like to approach and take the sadness away, but she clutches it to her. She will not share.

A breath in, a breath out. Sun recedes and the mountain's surface cools. Sun rises and a cloud lies down along the ridge. The mountain can see each molecule of water in it.

Some people spin on the mountain's crust without ever attaching. That woman there with the baby on her hip and three boys trailing behind. She has not had time to put down roots. It is all she can do not to fly off the surface. But others feel the mountain.

A girl stands studying the gorge. The mountain loves the earthy tone of her skin, the way she squints, memorizing fissures in the rock. She will be a woman soon and if she leaves this place, she will take the mountain with her. There is another child like this one somewhere, and the mountain sighs with her absence. It remembers a small-handed touch, tiny houses built of shards of stone, roofs of flaking mica.

A breath in, a breath out.

A woman works in a garden. From the house another woman calls her, delight in her voice, and slowly makes her way out the door with her walker. The first woman waits for her to maneuver down the stairs, then takes off her sweater and puts it around her lover's shoulders, hugging her close. Their laughter dissipates into air.

Nearby, a man prepares to walk on a string, the gorge open below him. He tests the tension of his cable, already thinking of the next town, the next crowd. Wind howls around him.

A breath in, a breath out.

At the school on the hill a father helps a small boy down from a wall. The mountain feels the man-made wall the way a human feels hair or fingernails, as an extension of itself. In the building in front of the wall, the headmaster closes his office door for the last time and leaves his keys hanging in the lock. He walks down the road with his hands in his pockets.

A breath in, a breath out. A breath in, a breath out. Headmasters come and go. Paint peels and is repainted. Buildings are taken down and new ones replace them. Parents who went to the school themselves bring their children to enroll. They remark on the changes, but it is the unchanged they breathe in when they stand on the newly built deck looking out at the mountain. In a field near the school an old dog stops and sniffs the wind, searching for someone he has lost, until the rustle of a rabbit turns memory to vapor. The mountain, too, feels a loss, someone missing.

A breath in, a breath out. A breath in, a breath out. Leaves turn from green to yellow to red and fall from the trees. They decay into dirt and work their way into the mountain's tiny crevices.

At a place where the mountain's stones elbow their way out of the ground, there is a noise in the woods. A man and woman walk with their little boy across a muddy creek bed. The woman is in front and reaches the far side of the creek first. The child starts to run after her, but the father grabs him by the waistband of his pants. "Let Mommy be by herself for a minute. You can play in the creek with me." He calls to his wife. "I've got him, Lorna."

The woman walks to the place where the stones jut out. A few gray strands shine in the brown hair she pushes back from her face. She is not old but the skin around her eyes is lined from a life of careful looking. The sun is out and she places her palm on the surface of the largest boulder to feel the warm stone under her hand.

The mountain knows that hand.

The woman speaks in a whisper, "*I'm back.*"

Something greater than joy swells within the mountain, humming along its ridges and down into the plateaus that stretch all the way to the sea.